"I heard you sold of some of the horses."

Aubrey nodded. "Damn near killed me to do it. But they brought in good money, and they cost money to feed. Daddy and Momma were angry with me for a week and didn't speak to me for two days… not one word. But they knew it had to be done. I used some of the money to pay down the debts and the rest to buy some more head that will bring in money down the road. It's hell being a small business, but I think, or at least I hope and pray, that we're on the right track now, 'cause if we're not, I don't know what more I can do except head off Daddy's buying more of what we don't need."

"It was no problem, and Bridger was giving your dad a break because they're friends, so I could give him a better price. Everybody came out ahead."

"Well, I'll remember what you did."

Garrett leaned a little closer. "I hope you'll remember this." He closed the distance between them until their lips touched and then sealed over each other. Aubrey closed his eyes and let the heat that out-sizzled the Texas summer run through him.

Andrew Grey

THE LONE
RANCHER

PUBLISHED BY

Published by
DREAMSPINNER PRESS

5032 Capital Circle SW, Suite 2, PMB# 279,
Tallahassee, FL 32305-7886 USA
www.dreamspinnerpress.com

ISBN: 978-1-63476-912-9
Digital ISBN: 978-1-63476-913-6
Library of Congress Control Number: 2015952693
Published February 2016
v. 1.0

Printed in the United States of America

ANDREW GREY grew up in western Michigan with a father who loved to tell stories and a mother who loved to read them. Since then he has lived all over the country and traveled throughout the world. He has a master's degree from the University of Wisconsin-Milwaukee and now works full-time on his writing. Andrew's hobbies include collecting antiques, gardening, and leaving his dirty dishes anywhere but in the sink (particularly when writing). He considers himself blessed with an accepting family, fantastic friends, and the world's most supportive and loving husband. Andrew currently lives in beautiful historic Carlisle, Pennsylvania.

E-mail: andrewgrey@comcast.net

Website: www.andrewgreybooks.com

To Dana Piazzi and all my fans. I write my stories for you.

Also to B.A. and Lew for showing me around Greenville and introducing this Northerner to real Texas hospitality.

Chapter One

AUBREY Klein sat back in his chair with a groan. No matter how many ways he tried to add up these damned numbers, they just wouldn't come out right. The ranch was doing better, and he'd made a lot of progress in the last six months, but they were still hanging on by a lick and a prayer. The hole that had been dug in over years couldn't be filled in and wiped clean in a matter of months, he knew. The debt was going down, and if he had to, he could hold on for maybe another six months to a year, as long as he caught some sort of break with the weather. He closed the ledger with a thud and wished his daddy had converted the records to computer years ago. Of course, if he'd have done that, he might have done some of the other things necessary to keep the ranch from ending up on the brink of foreclosure.

"Son, are you done in there? I need your help in the yard."

"Sure, Dad, I'll be right there," Aubrey called. There was work to be done, and wishing the ranch books were in better shape wasn't going to make it happen. That was going to take hard work and sacrifice. Aubrey cringed as he thought about the sacrifices he'd already made. But if those sacrifices saved the ranch and helped his mom and dad get back on a level footing, it would be worth it.

He got up and left the office. For years this room had been his father's domain, but now it was his. Aubrey met his dad by the kitchen and followed him outside, where a load of hay for the horses was waiting to be unloaded. Aubrey groaned. "Where did this come from?" He clamped his eyes closed. They already had a barn full of hay.

"John Bridger had some extra, and we always need hay, so…."

"Dad." Aubrey stifled the urge to yell. It wouldn't do any good. Diabetes and its complications had slowly robbed his father of the ability to fully think things through, and he now tended to make emotional decisions as opposed to business or rational ones. "The barn's already full. There's enough hay to more than last us."

Dad walked to the barn and peered upward. Aubrey could see his father's shoulders slump slightly the moment he realized Aubrey was right, and just like that Aubrey wished he hadn't been. "Sorry, son, I thought…." His words trailed off in a cloud of defeat. "Nothing seems to turn out right for me anymore."

"Don't worry about it, Dad. I'll find a place for it. Just be sure to ask me before you buy things for the ranch. I have things under control, and we're going to be okay." Lord, he hoped to high heaven that he wasn't telling his dad a lie. Things were getting better, and he was close to having the money together to finally pay off the most vicious of the loans his father had taken out. Once that debt was gone, he hoped to be able to start paying down the others and free up some money for improvements. "Why don't you go on in and see what Mom has for lunch? I need to get this unloaded." Aubrey looked at his watch and realized he needed to get a move on, or he was going to be late.

"Everything okay?" Garrett Lamston asked as he came around the barn. He worked for Bridger and had obviously been the one to make the delivery. "You don't need this hay, do you?"

Aubrey waited until his dad was inside. "No. I have plenty right now. I know with the drought the past few months that there are plenty of folks who need it. But I—" The last thing he needed was another bill for something he didn't need.

"Don't you worry. John offered his extra to your dad because he wanted to make sure you had enough. We have a number of places that will take it." Garrett smiled, and Aubrey did his best not to let his heart do the little flips it always did when Garrett was nearby. Not that it mattered. He and Garrett were friends—or at least they'd known each other since they were kids. "It's not a problem."

"That's mighty good of you," Aubrey said with relief.

"I take it things are still tough for your dad." Garrett lifted his hat and wiped his forehead before dropping the old, once-white Stetson back down onto his head.

He'd worn that same hat for years, and it looked as fine on him today as always.

"They aren't going to get better. All those years on insulin and not listening to the doctors have taken their toll. Momma does what she can, but he's a stubborn old coot and overdoes it all the time. Last week I found him passed out on the barn floor after he tried to clean stalls and overexerted himself." He'd had to use glucose injections to bring his father around. It hadn't been pretty, but he'd done what he had to.

Garrett nodded slowly in that way he had. "Wish there was something I could do to help."

Aubrey patted the trailer. "You already have."

Garrett smiled and turned to go. Aubrey watched him as he went, glad he was alone, because anyone watching him stare at that high, pert cowboy ass in those tight Wranglers would know exactly what kind of thoughts and images were running around in his head. He blinked to clear his lascivious thoughts and school his expression as Garrett climbed in the truck. While things were changing—maybe slowly in this part of Texas—he wasn't about to tempt fate and let everyone know which way he swung. With the ranch just hanging on, the last thing he needed was rumors and folks deciding they didn't need to be doing business with him. That could be the end of everything he'd been working so hard to preserve.

Aubrey raised his hand in a combination farewell and thank-you. Garrett opened the window, leaning out so Aubrey got a look at just his head and broad shoulders. "We should go for a beer sometime. Give me a call the next time you're going to town, and I'll meet you."

"I'll buy the first round," Aubrey called and swallowed hard as Garrett stared back at him for a second longer than necessary. Heat rose in Aubrey's stomach as that itchy feeling filled his belly and the tingle of potential possibilities buzzed in his head. He blinked and was about to turn away when Garrett pulled his head back into the truck and thunked the door closed. A hand jutted out the window, and the truck and trailer started pulling down the drive. Aubrey inhaled deeply, wondering if he'd really seen what he thought. It had to be his imagination. He'd known Garrett for years, and there had never been any indication in all that time that Garrett was interested in bulls rather than heifers.

With one small crisis averted, Aubrey pulled his attention away from the possible contents of Garrett's jeans and turned toward the house.

"Did you get the hay unloaded already?" his dad asked from his favorite recliner in the living room when Aubrey got out of the oppressive heat and into the air-conditioned comfort of the house.

"Bridger offered it to us because he wanted to make sure we were doing okay. There are other folks who need it a lot worse, so they're going to sell it to them." He patted his dad's shoulder lightly. "We're going to be okay, and it's all good."

"Okay, then…." His dad put his feet up, and Aubrey figured he'd probably be asleep in five minutes or less.

"You ready to eat?" his mom asked as she came in from the kitchen. She'd aged a lot over the past few years, just like his dad. Her hair was mostly gray now instead of the raven black he remembered from when he was younger. Unlike his father, she was in good health, but taking care of Dad had taken its toll on her.

"That'd be great. I need to leave in an hour or so." He checked his watch.

"Going to Dallas again to see your friends?" she asked without judgment or reproach.

"Yeah." He sat at the table and hung his hat on the back of the chair next to him.

"You need to get away every now and then. Everything here will be fine while you're gone." She got plates and dished up some of her special macaroni salad and added a huge, thick sandwich on homemade bread. None of that store-bought "sawdust bread," as she called it. Mom did things the old-fashioned way whenever she could, but it was getting harder and harder on her. All Aubrey wanted to do was make his mom and dad's lives easier, and he'd do whatever he had to in order to make that happen.

"This is really good," he told her, not really wanting to talk too much about his weekly trips into Dallas to see his "friends." The less he said, the fewer lies he told, and when it came to his momma, that was always a good thing. "You always take good care of us." He took another bite of the roast beef sandwich and sighed to himself.

"You're the one taking care of us now," she said. She looked into the other room.

"Did he eat?"

"Yeah. He was hungry, so I fed him as soon as he came in," she whispered. "He ate, then went to sit in his chair and fell asleep." She turned away and sat down with her own plate. His mom had always been the last one to eat. "I heard from Carolann this morning. She said she's been real busy in San Francisco with her work and all."

Aubrey nodded and tried not to let jealousy and bitterness well up. His sister always had excuses not to come home and help out. Aubrey took another bite of his sandwich to stifle a growl. Part of the reason they were all in this mess was because his dad had taken out a loan against the ranch to help pay for her Stanford education.

"She said she sent out a check to start paying us back."

Aubrey lowered his head and tried not to humph. Somehow the postal service always seemed to lose Carolann's checks. "That's good." There was no use arguing. Mom wouldn't hear it. Carolann was her only daughter, just like he was her only son, and Momma wasn't going to hear bad things said about either of her children. Besides, Aubrey knew the loan had been their decision, and what was done was done. "When I get back, I'm going to put in that new electric line out to the barn. That way I can bury the cable and get rid of that old overhead line."

"You need me to do anything for you while you're gone?"

"Just make sure Dad feeds and waters the horses. I got everything set out in the barn, so it'll be easy on him. He needs to do it tonight and tomorrow morning. I'll be back in the afternoon and can take over from there."

She flashed him a disgusted look. "We've been doing this work for—"

Aubrey put up his hand to keep her from getting up a head of steam. "I was only trying to help." Aubrey looked to the living room. "He bought a trailer load of hay we didn't need," he added in a whisper. "I took care of it, but I'm worried."

The fire in her eyes died. "I am too." Her voice was little more than a whisper and filled with pain and worry. He hated the strain all this was taking on her.

"We'll take care of things here." She took his plate when he was done. "Go on and have some fun. You work hard, so you deserve it. Give yourself a chance to let off some steam with your friends, and I'll see you tomorrow."

Aubrey stood and kissed his mom on the cheek. Then he strode down to his room and grabbed the small bag he had packed and ready. He carried it out to his truck and then did one last check that everything was all set before he got in the truck and pulled down the drive for the ride from Greenville to Dallas.

Chapter Two

"LADIES, gentlemen, and those of you who have yet to make up your minds," the master of ceremonies quipped over the loudspeaker. It was an old joke, and one Aubrey had heard each and every Saturday night. Activity buzzed around him, but Aubrey kept his mind focused on the task at hand. "We have an amazing lineup for you tonight." A whoop went up from the gathered crowd, shaking the walls. "And we all know who you're waiting for…."

Another, louder yell made the floor vibrate. Excitement ramped up inside him, and Aubrey took a step closer to the stage entrance. He knew the shtick that went on—it was all designed to get the crowd fired up.

"Should I bring him out at the end of the show?"

The resulting sound was deafening. "Now!"

"I can't hear you," he sang, and the crowd became even louder. "All right, you asked for him, and here he is. The one… the only… the cowboy who can light my prairie on fire anytime he wants. The Lone Rancher!"

Music pumped, and the stage went dark as Aubrey raced on. When the lights flashed on, the crowd of men in front of him went wild. He snapped his hips to one side, and men yelled, jumping up and down to the beat of the music. He began to move, pumping his fists and snapping his hips to the beat in a raucous, salacious impersonation of ass-slapping sex, the fringe on his chaps flapping wildly. Then he turned around to give them a clear view of his jeans-clad ass framed in chaps and pumped his hips, clenching his cheeks, making them do a little dance that sent the crowd into a frenzy.

His vest was the first to go. Aubrey peeled it away, twirling it over his head as he rolled his hips, moving his entire body to the pounding beat that filled him. He knew his routines by heart, so he let go, sinking deep into himself and just going with what felt good. He kicked his boots into the wings and then removed the chaps in a flash of leather that sailed across the stage, landing just out of sight of the crowd. Now in just his checked shirt, jeans, hat, and, of course, the mask he wore the entire time he was in the club, he whirled around, his back to the crowd, and pulled at his shirt, spreading it wide, letting it slip off his shoulders. He shimmied it back and forth, then whipped back to face the audience, pulling the shirt closed as he did.

Their energy coursed through him, sending ripples of sexual energy streaming up his back to his head and then shooting downward, his skin pricking and the hair on his arms and legs standing on end, he felt so alive. He pulled open his shirt once again, dropping it away, flexing his chest to the whistles and yells. Aubrey fell back on his hands and then jumped to his feet, repeating the move and ending with his hands on the floor, thrusting his hips toward the ceiling to the delight of the crowd.

The music slowed just a little, shifting to a quasi-line-dancing beat. He leaped to his feet, rocking on his legs, hands just above his oversized sparkly belt buckle, accentuating his crotch, swaying his hips. The crowd was going wild, shaking and vibrating en masse in front of him. Men had their hands up, beating the air as he stepped around, meeting the eyes of various guys, winking at them, playing the game, flirting outrageously. As the music built, the tension in the crowd rose to a peak, and at the exact beat, he tugged. His tight pants ripped free, and he tossed them away.

In the tiniest of thongs that left nothing to the imagination, he stepped down off the stage and out into the crowd. A sea of bills popped into the air, and he collected them slowly, one at a time, tucking them into his pouch. He got a few grabs and gropes—that came with the territory, along with the money—and when the music finally died as the last bills were stuffed home, the Lone Rancher, wearing only a thong, a mask, and a smile, climbed back to the stage, turned, and gave them a farewell hip thrust.

That's when Aubrey saw him, second row off to the right. Garrett stood right there, eyes glued to him. Aubrey was covered in sweat, but he was instantly cold, a bone-deep chill so ferocious he wondered if he'd ever get warm again. He gave a final wave and hurried off the stage, stumbling down the steps in order to get away.

"Fuck," he groaned when he made it back to the changing area and began pulling the bills from everywhere they'd been stuffed. Part of the trick was to do it carefully so he didn't end up with paper cuts anywhere important.

A bottle of water was placed on the table in front of him by one of the stage guys as he hurried by. Aubrey didn't see who it was; he was too preoccupied with the fact that Garrett had been out front. Well, that answered one question, but it raised a hell of a lot more. Did Garrett know who he was? God, he sure as hell hoped not. His heart raced, and he grabbed the bottle, gulping down the water as one of the other guys brought him the clothes he'd stripped off.

"You looked really good," Hank the Hunk told him, handing him the stack with a flip of his long blond mane. "They always go for you."

"It's the mask," Aubrey answered. He only took it off in the club when he was alone in the bathroom and needed to wipe his face. Otherwise, none of the guys knew what he looked like, and for the most part they all respected his privacy. They all had things about their lives they didn't want spread around.

"Are you doing the next show?" Hank asked as he stepped into a pair of fireman's pants and then pulled on a fire coat before slapping a fire helmet on his head.

"Yes. I only get here on Saturdays, so I try to do both shows." Aubrey was feeling much more normal. The sweat that had built up while he was on stage had evaporated, and he was hydrated once again. He began dressing in his costume for his second appearance in the show, where all the guys would dance together. When he was ready, he went to stand in the wings. Usually he watched the other guys to see if there was anything new he could learn, but this time his gaze was drawn to the audience, where he could see Garrett. He seemed to be watching the show only part of the time and craning his head around the rest of the time.

Aubrey was getting ready to go back on when he saw Garrett weave his way back through the crowd, and he breathed a small sigh of relief. Maybe Garrett was getting ready to leave for the night? He sure as hell hoped so.

"Gentlemen, letches, and perverts everywhere, it's time for the finale, so let's bring out *all the boys*!" The club plunged into darkness, and they all took their places. Then the lights strobed on, and they went into their routine. Shirts and pants came off in unison, working the crowd into a frenzy. The music built, and the taller guys bent over so the smaller guys could roll over their backs, legs in the air for three beats, and then they were all on their feet, hips gyrating in unison, chests pumping, playing up all their "assets." The music reached a crescendo, and then the lights went dark. When the music stopped, the walls shook as the men applauded, pounding their feet on the floor. Aubrey and the others hurried off stage as the master of ceremonies thanked everyone for coming.

They all got a rest while the crowd filed out, and the club was cleaned up so it could get ready for the second, longer, and more expensive show of the night. Aubrey dressed and left the club so he could get some fresh air.

He stepped out of the back door into a night that felt as though he were breathing soup. Aubrey looked up at the sky and hoped the rain he was smelling on the air was going north through home.

"You're the Lone Rancher, right?"

Aubrey knew that voice and turned around slowly. "Yeah," he said, lowering his voice slightly and hoping it didn't sound too fake. Garrett would know his voice in an instant.

"You were really awesome," Garrett said. "Are you a real cowboy?" He leaned closer, and Aubrey's heart stopped. He saw recognition in Garrett's eyes and figured the gig was up. "You are. You have the calluses and cuts to prove it." Garrett whistled. "I'm a cowboy too, but you'd never catch me up there doing what you're doing. I can't dance, for one thing, and if I met a guy I liked, I don't know how I could tell him I was taking my clothes off in front of strangers. Is that why you wear the mask? So you can deny what you're doing later?"

Aubrey ground his teeth. "No. I do it to keep my privacy."

"Folks at home don't know you're gay, huh?" He smiled. "Don't worry, me neither. It's hard in the Bible Belt, I get that." Garrett looked like he was getting ready to leave, and Aubrey wished he would. He wasn't going to tell him that he was dancing in order to try to save his family's ranch. The more information he gave, the greater the chance he'd give Garrett some piece of information that would kick in recognition. "Do you… you know… spend time with guys after the club closes?" Garrett asked. "Because if you do, I think I'd love to spend time with you." The heat in Garrett's eyes was attractive as hell, and it took all Aubrey's willpower to shake his head.

"I dance and that's all. There are plenty of other guys who will be happy to spend time with you, I'm sure." His teeth grated at the thought of Garrett going home with some other guy, but he'd never done that, and he wasn't going to start now, even though he'd been interested in Garrett for as long as he could remember. Nothing was going to come of it anyway, especially after what Garrett had said tonight.

"I take it your folks don't know what you're doing?" Garrett said, as though he'd stumbled onto something important.

Before he could stop his head from moving, he'd nodded. The thought of what his momma and dad would say if they knew what he did every Saturday night was enough to make him sick. The way he figured it, if he could do this for another few months, he'd have the bulk of the debt paid off, and then he could hang up the Lone Rancher, and that would be that. No one would ever need to be the wiser—not his family, not the people in town. He'd been doing well, too, and now here was Garrett standing near him. Thank God it was dark and people only saw what they wanted to see.

"I need to get back inside." He turned and pulled open the door. It was the cowardly way out, but he needed to get away. "I'll see you 'round." Aubrey stepped inside and willed himself not to take one last look, but damned if he didn't turn around anyway.

Garrett's eyes burned into him, heat and desire shining like a beacon across the darkness. He'd been caught looking, and he stopped, staring, Garrett's fire sending electric shocks running through him. How many times had he wanted Garrett to look at him like that? But that heat and passion was directed at a man who was, as far as Garrett knew, a stranger. He couldn't deny his attraction, but the mask he wore effectively ensured that Garrett had no idea who he was. Hell, it could have been the whole mask thing that was getting Garrett's motor running in the first place.

Aubrey had to put an end to this. He turned away first, letting the door close, shutting out Garrett along with the oppressive heat and humidity.

"You look like someone just kicked your cat," Hank said when Aubrey joined the others in the dressing area ten minutes later, after he'd stopped in the restroom to take off his mask and throw some water on his face to cool himself down. The crowds and the excitement usually got him going, but that was nothing compared to what Garrett had done to him with just one single look.

"Nah." He did his best to lighten his voice and pull his mind away from Garrett's smoldering heat. "Just something strange going on." He looked around. "Where's Simon?"

"Making a little extra on the outside...." Hank raised his eyebrows. "A guy knocked on the door a little while ago, looking for you. I said you had stepped out. He came back a few minutes ago and asked if he could talk to the police officer. Apparently he'd been bad and was in need of some serious correction." He grinned at his own joke.

Well, that told him plenty about Garrett's interest. He was just horny, and while Aubrey might have been his first choice, he'd moved on to Simon quickly enough. "Okay."

"If you were interested, you should have said something. I know you don't do that sort of thing, so I didn't think anything about putting the guy off you and onto Simon." Hank moved on, and Aubrey wondered if the guy they were talking about was indeed Garrett or if he'd been jumping to conclusions. Not that it mattered. Even if Garrett was interested in him as Aubrey, and there had certainly been no indication of that in God knows how many years, it didn't matter what Garrett felt. He'd made it perfectly clear that he might be interested in a dancer for some quick fun, but nothing more.

"The show will start in thirty minutes," Barry said, already dressed in his tuxedo—without a shirt, of course. "I'm going to change the order tonight. Lone Rancher, I want you on last. They always go nuts, and so many of them are coming in to see you that I want them hot, shaking, and drinking as much as possible before you go on. We're going to lead with Hank, and then…." He looked around. "Go find Simon and get his dick out of whatever mouth he found to stick it in," he said, looking at Mike. "And be sure to tell him that if he's late for a before-show meeting again, I'll kick him out of here on his high, tight ass."

Aubrey kept a straight face. He had one more show to do, and then he could go back to his hotel, sleep, and drive home in the morning, hopefully with a thousand dollars in his pocket. He already had nearly half that from what he'd gathered after his first performance and what he got as part of the tips gathered at the end of the show. The second show was longer, and the patrons had usually had a drink or two before they arrived. Then, after a little warm-up, the crowd was raring to go. The one drawback was that by going last, he could find the crowd with little money left, but if he was lucky they would have saved up, and he could get the bulk of what they'd brought with them.

"Ladies, gentlemen, and those of you who have yet to make up your minds…." The show began, and tonight Barry made sure to explain the rules in his usual banter, but he was very clear. Then, of course, his duty done, he brought out Hank and proceeded to demonstrate exactly where the patrons could touch and where they couldn't. That bit always went over big, especially when Barry made a show of grabbing Hank's crotch and fanning himself as though he was about to be overcome by the vapors. "Now that you understand where you can't touch and where you can…." Barry reached out, and Hank snapped his hands over his crotch. It was always funny, but Aubrey didn't need to see it. This was standard, and he'd heard it so many times he could do the bit from memory.

Aubrey waited his turn, congratulating the other guys and sharing in their excitement. Of course, as soon as he was done, Simon disappeared for a while, most likely to make one lucky fan very happy. Before it was his turn to go on, Aubrey peered out, surveying the crowd. He didn't see Garrett, and he couldn't decide if that was good or not. He figured if he was out front for the next show, then it was unlikely Garrett had been the guy who'd been interested in Simon earlier. But if he was gone, then Aubrey wasn't going to have to worry about him seeing his act and having something trigger who he was.

Thankfully, when his turn came, he didn't see Garrett, though that didn't mean he wasn't there. The place was packed, after all. He danced to "Save a Horse, Ride a Cowboy," which took on a whole new meaning when he ended the dance in nothing but a jockstrap with a cowboy hat on it. He made his rounds of the crowd and ended up palming some of the bills to keep them from falling out.

After the final number, he hurried to the back, gathered all his money and costumes, dressed, and left the club by the back door. He got into his truck and drove back to his hotel. When he got out, he remembered he was still wearing his mask. He unfastened it and lowered it from his face.

"Aubrey!" It was Garrett, and he was coming toward him.

Chapter Three

AUBREY still had his mask in his hand. If Garrett saw it, his secret was out. He balled his fist and shoved the fabric into his pocket. "Garrett, what are you doing here?"

"I was going to ask you the same thing." Garrett looked around nervously, as though he'd been caught doing something he shouldn't have.

"I was visiting some friends, and we decided to go out for a drink. It got a little later than usual. I was just about to hit the hay." He stroked his brow to wipe away the sweat. "I have to head home pretty early in the morning so I don't leave Mom and Dad with all the feeding and watering chores."

"I was just in town for some fun." Garrett moved closer, and Aubrey glanced behind him. Some of his costume pieces were lying out on the seat. He stepped away from the truck and closed the door, dousing the interior light and hopefully hiding the incriminating evidence.

Aubrey suppressed a smile. He knew what kind of fun Garrett had been interested in, but he couldn't let on about it. However, the heat in Garrett's eyes was enticing. He knew Garrett was interested in men— well, the Lone Rancher knew, even if Aubrey wasn't supposed to. That bit of information gave him a sense of power, but it also made his stomach roil at the same time. If he said one word he shouldn't, he could blow his entire situation. The money he had in his pockets would see the ranch through the next week and help get them further out of the hole. The income wasn't something he could do without.

"Did you find what you were looking for?" Aubrey asked.

"Nope," Garrett breathed, and Aubrey wondered what that meant. The heavy scent of alcohol on Garrett's breath reached his nose, and he wrinkled it slightly. "I went out for a while, and I was hoping to see this gu… girl, but h… she… aww, hell." Garrett turned away. "You can hate me if you want, but I hate this shit." He kicked at the stones on the tarmac. "I was at this club where they have these guys, and they…. See, I wasn't here for no girl." Garrett looked ready to crumble like a house of cards. "I caught a ride down here with a friend and then hurried over there." He pointed in the general direction of the club.

"So you don't have a ride?"

"I was supposed to meet him an hour ago, but he'd already left. His momma called, so he had to get right back, and I couldn't very well tell him where I was, so I said to go and I'd get back on my own. I was going to try to find a room, but they're full up. I figured I'd get to the bus station in the morning." He looked so dog-kicked that Aubrey couldn't not help him.

"I got a room here. You can stay with me, and I'll give you a ride back in the morning." What the hell else was he going to do?

"You aren't mad… or disgusted?" Garrett asked.

"Fuck," Aubrey groaned. The worry in Garrett's eyes wrapped tightly around his heart. He knew that worry so damn well, like it was his constant companion. "No, I'm not mad or anything. Why would I be?" His stomach roiled again, and he thought he was going to be sick, but if Garrett could be brave enough to be truthful, at least he could come part of the way. "That would be like the pot calling the kettle black, if you know what I mean." Aubrey pulled out his wallet and handed Garrett one of his key cards. "It's room 212. Go on up, and I'll get my stuff and follow you."

Garrett seemed shocked as shit. His mouth hung open as he took the key card, hand moving in a kind of slow motion. Then he grinned, and Aubrey wondered what in the hell that meant. "Thanks." He took the card and walked toward the hotel door, shoulders set a little straighter.

Aubrey waited until he was out of sight before pulling open the truck door and gathering his costume. He folded it and placed it in the bag, then put it deep behind the seat. He remembered his mask in his pocket and added it to the bag. Then he put the seat back into place and snatched his overnight bag before heading into the hotel. This was going to be a very long night, and he was quite possibly going to regret extending his offer, but he couldn't leave Garrett hanging even if it was going to put them in close proximity with only one bed.

He walked slowly to his room, wondering what he was going to find. Of course, his imagination was on overdrive as he conjured up images of Garrett lying naked on the bed, waiting for him. The thing was… he liked that idea a lot. Garrett was wiry, strong, and lean from years of hard work. Many times he'd checked out what his friend had stuffed in his jeans, but only when he thought he could get away with it.

He slid the card into the slot and pushed open the door. Garrett sat on the edge of the bed, very much dressed, holding his head in his hands. "Man, what am I going to do?"

"About what?" Aubrey asked as he closed the door. "You're a little drunk, and things have been hard."

"What can I tell my folks?" Garrett asked. "A deacon and his wife are never going to understand how this can be possible." He looked up in misery. "I tried to deny it and push it away. I used to pray all the time for God to make me like everyone else."

"I don't think it works that way. See, the way I look at it, you either like girls or you don't." Aubrey shrugged. He'd accepted that he was gay a while ago, and he was honest with himself. He knew it was hypocritical to keep quiet about it, but it was also a case of survival, for him and for the ranch… as well as Mom and Dad. "There's nothing you can 'do' about it." Aubrey dropped his bag. He was tired, way too tired for soul searching and hand wringing tonight. He needed to get in bed and fall asleep. The dancing and performing took a lot out of him. He was used to hard work, but that was something else.

"Sorry about all this," Garrett said.

He placed his hand on Garrett's shoulder and was surprised when Garrett put a hand on top of it. "We've been friends forever," he reminded Garrett. "It don't matter to me if you're gay. And for the record, if I was straight, it wouldn't matter either. You work hard and do good for Bridger. He's lucky to have you, and let me tell you this: cows, steers, bulls, and horses don't give a fiddler's fuck about who you sleep with. The rest ain't nobody's business."

"Do the friends you were out drinking with know you're gay?" Garrett asked.

Aubrey wasn't sure what to tell him, but he decided that no answer was better than a lie. "You need to get ready for bed. So take the bathroom first." Aubrey reached in his bag and tossed Garrett a bottle of Scope. "For God's sake, use it, because I'm not smelling your nasty-assed breath all night long." He turned away and waited for Garrett to go into the bathroom. Then he used the privacy to change, hoping he could get the damned thing he was wearing off and hidden before Garrett came back out.

Aubrey found a T-shirt and a pair of gym shorts. He'd just finished pulling those on when Garrett came out in nothing but his boxers, carrying the rest of his clothes. "God, these things stink of cigarettes."

"Then leave them in the bathroom so they don't stink up the entire room. You'll have to wear them home, but maybe they can air out some." Aubrey took his turn in the bathroom and then turned out the light and climbed into bed.

He heard Garrett sighing like Christ on the cross, as his momma would say.

"Just let it go and get some sleep. There ain't nothing so bad that it's going to bring on the end of the world." What Aubrey wanted was pretty simple: to be able to sleep and get back home, where he could get some more bills paid and hope like hell nothing had fallen off the rails while he was gone.

"Have you been… you know, with other guys?" Garrett asked.

Aubrey groaned softly as he rolled over. "This ain't high school, where we get to see who gets the most action."

"I've been with girls," Garrett said. "I tried really hard."

"Weren't you supposed to marry Lynn Mumford?" Aubrey remembered the talk.

"That was her running her mouth off. She was all kinds of interested and tried to get me to propose. She even went so far as to try to get me to have a go at her. Turned out she was pregnant with someone else's kid, and she was looking for a daddy for him. Cute little boy too. I go see them a lot. She and I are friends now, and she's dating a rancher with a place north of town. Looks like he's going to marry her, so it all turned out for the best."

"I guess it did," Aubrey mumbled as sleep crept up on him. "Would you have called it off?"

"I never proposed. She was all talk, but I wasn't going to go through with it. That wouldn't be fair… to her or me. Though I'd be lying if I said I never thought about it." Garrett rolled over, the bed rocking a little. "Sometimes I think it would have been so easy to get married and be normal. But the thing is, I didn't love her."

"Yeah, I can understand that. My mom was pushing fillies in front of me for a while, but I was always too busy, or that's how I made it look. Truth was, I was scared to death of them. Never much knew what to do or how to act."

"I get that. Like they're china dolls or something. Pretty to look at, but they'll break if we play with them." Garrett grew quiet for a while, and Aubrey hoped he'd gone to sleep. "I like things a little more active… if you know what I mean." Garrett let his hand run up Aubrey's side.

It felt good to be touched. He quivered but didn't move. This was a bad idea, and while Garrett had already seen him mostly naked as the Lone Rancher, he couldn't allow him to see him as Aubrey. A body wasn't a body, no matter what anybody said.

"You feel so warm," Garrett breathed into his ear. "I haven't been with anyone in a long time."

"What about…?" he began before stopping himself. He couldn't admit to seeing Garrett at the club or to being propositioned. Or the fact that he thought Garrett had been with Simon. Aubrey stiffened, and Garrett's hand stilled and then slipped away.

"What about what?" Garrett snapped. "You were going to say something."

Aubrey hesitated, at a loss for words. "Nothing," he said quietly.

"I won't touch you again." His voice was getting slurry, and Aubrey figured the last drinks Garrett had had must be hitting his system. "We're friends, and that's more important than one night of—" Garrett giggled. "You know…."

"We are friends, have been for a long time, but I think we're learning some more about each other." Aubrey closed his eyes and blurted out what he wanted to say. "It will be nice to have a friend back home who understands." *God, would it ever.* The thought of being less alone….

Garrett turned toward him and slung an arm around his waist. Aubrey groaned and shifted closer, giving

Garrett the green light. He wanted to be close, and it was dark in here. He'd been dancing for months now with his eyes only on the money. He never went home with anyone or let them touch him. There were many times he'd been ready to burst, and Garrett's hand on his belly had his stomach doing little flips.

He knew this was a bad idea on so many levels, but his logical brain was shutting down. Physically he was on fire—his legs ached, and the embers that had been banked for so dang long had been coaxed to life in a big way.

Garrett's hand stopped moving, and Aubrey stilled as well, wondering what was going to happen next. "Garrett," he whispered and slowly rolled over. A gentle snore reached his ears, and Aubrey sighed softly, making sure he was all right. Garrett rolled away from him onto his side, and Aubrey wanted to scream. Well, this was for the best. He rolled over as well, punching his pillow and shaking the bed roughly.

It must have jarred Garrett, because he rolled over again and pressed right up against him, putting his arm around his waist again. The soft snoring continued, though, and Aubrey groaned under his breath. At the start of this little adventure with Garrett, all he'd wanted was the chance to get a decent night's sleep, but Garrett's hands, the smallest touch—like the way his fingers moved ever so gently against his belly, even in his sleep—sent little tendrils of molten heat through him. What the hell was he going to do besides stay awake half the night listening to Garrett snore?

Chapter Four

"DO you want me to drop you at Bridger's?"

Garrett nodded as he sat staring out the side window of Aubrey's truck. "I'd appreciate it." That was the most he had spoken the entire morning.

Aubrey gripped the wheel, his knuckles turning white. "What the hell is wrong with you? I was good enough to put you up last night." To say nothing of spending the night with a monumental case of blue balls. But looking back, it was good that nothing had happened between them. They could go on as friends. Well, they could as long as Garrett stopped being an asshole.

"Last night… I… I said things that I haven't told anyone, and…."

"So what? I know what you said, and it's no big deal. Remember, I told you the same thing."

Garrett nodded. "I can't remember much about what happened last night, and then this morning I woke up with you in my arms, and…. Well, I don't want to fuck up our friendship. It's too important to me."

Aubrey rolled his eyes. "Nothing happened last night, you big pussy. You tried to get something going and then fell asleep. If you want to be sorry about something, then you could try being sorry for spending the entire night snoring in my ear." He kept quiet about waking this morning with a sizable erection pressing to his ass. It looked as though that was a memory he'd keep to himself. "I already told you, nothing is going to change our friendship. So stop being such a dick and go back to normal." Aubrey pulled to a stop near the turn.

Garrett turned and smiled tentatively. "You sure it's okay?"

"Hell, yes. Nothing has changed. We're friends, and we'll always be friends, so stop worrying. And while you're at it, grow yourself a set of balls."

"Well… last night I swear someone was checking out my set of balls, so you know I have them."

Aubrey shook his head. "Then use them." He winked, and Garrett laughed full-out.

"Sometimes I think things will never be normal, but then you give me crap like you always do, and I know everything is going to be okay."

"Of course it is." He moved the truck forward and made the turn into Bridger's drive. He pulled up near the bunkhouse and waited while Garrett got out. "I'll see you later in the week. Maybe we could get together for a beer." Garrett waved as he walked across the yard. Aubrey knew he should turn around and head home, but damn, the view was irresistible. He waited until

Garrett was out of sight, then pulled away and drove the few miles down the road to home.

As soon as he got out, he went right into the barn to check on the animals. Everything looked good, so he jogged inside.

"How was your trip?" his mom asked from where she sat on the sofa, knitting and watching television. His dad was in his usual spot, watching along with her. It seemed so strange to see them spending the day this way. His entire life they had been as active and busy as anyone he'd ever met.

"It was nice. Is everything okay here?" He set down the bag, plopping himself next to his mother. He didn't pay attention to the rerun of *Antiques Roadshow* they were watching, but instead kept looking at them, wondering and worrying just how long he was going to have both of them in his life.

"Do we need any feed? Hodgkins said he could hook us up with some."

"We're fine, Dad. Thanks." He sighed and was relieved that his father had asked before he'd acted. Thanks to another of his father's deals, they had enough feed for a month yet, which he was still trying to use up. In the end that deal had worked out really well, but Aubrey didn't want a repeat.

"What did you do in Dallas?" his mother asked. "I hope you didn't cause any trouble."

"When have I ever done that?" he asked innocently.

He got a stern look as his answer. "Don't make me recall the entire list. We'll be here till doomsday," his mother said. She remained serious for about two seconds, and then she smiled and shook her head.

"I was fine. No fights or anything," Aubrey said. "We went out last night and had some fun. That's all."

"I'd like to meet these friends of yours sometime. We should have a big cookout the way we used to when you were kids. Get your sister to come out, invite everybody."

Aubrey groaned. While those cookouts were legendary, and his parents spared little expense, they were also part of the reason they were in this mess. "How about we wait until things are doing better," he suggested. The weariness was seeping further and further into his bones. "We're just getting to the cusp of turning things around, and I don't want to have to have another meeting at the bank." Lord knew another of those wouldn't go as well as the last one. They had made no bones that the revised payments had to be made, or they were going to foreclose. So far he'd made every one, and he'd even been able to get them ahead. But using the cash reserves he'd built up on a party wouldn't be a good business decision.

"Nonsense. We should do what we used to do. The ranch is doing well with you running it, and we need to show our neighbors that we aren't down and out." She made things sound so reasonable, and Aubrey could see his father getting ready to agree.

"Not this year. Let me make sure we're solid first." He needed something to give and soon. "There's only so many messes I can clean up."

"Listen to Aubrey, Helen. He knows what we can and can't do." He reached across the distance between where they were sitting and took her hand. "If it weren't for him, we'd be out on the street. Things are different now. We can't do what we used to." He'd always tried to make her happy. It was one of the things Aubrey admired about his dad so very much. But Aubrey was also sure that it was the source of part of their troubles.

She nodded and went back to watching the television, the two of them still holding hands. Aubrey breathed a sigh of relief and stood, quietly leaving the room to give them their privacy.

In his own bedroom, with the door shut, Aubrey pulled the cash out of the side pocket of his bag and counted it. Yesterday had been a good day as far as money was concerned, even if he was turned around with this whole thing with Garrett. He knew it would be best to keep his distance for a while and just get through the next few months. By then, if things kept up, he'd be able to quit dancing and could go back to being just a cowboy again. The secrets and the lies could end, and maybe he could look at himself in the mirror in the mornings without seeing the darkness that always seemed to be there, just out of reach.

He added the money to the lockbox he kept in the back of his closet and put it away. Then he stripped off his clothes and got in the shower, trying to wash off the remnants of the night before. God, he tried to remember how he'd gotten himself into this mess, but it was all a blur of sleep deprivation and an unwillingness to want to dredge all that up again. Things were what they were.

As he reached for the soap and slicked his hands, he tried not to think of anything in particular, but it had been so good to have Garrett holding him, and the feel of his thickness pressing to his backside got him going from zero to sixty faster than any Corvette ever made. He closed his eyes and let the glimpse he'd gotten of Garrett in his boxers play in his head. Of course he began filling in the details, and soon Garrett had him on the bed, kissing, feeling, holding him, pressing him down with his delicious weight and heat. It didn't take long before Aubrey was right on the edge, holding himself there as long as he could, letting his fantasy give him what he desperately wanted but knew it was a bad idea to start wishing for or reaching out to take. Garrett had made his thoughts pretty clear outside the club, but Aubrey's libido didn't care, and as soon as he pushed the doubts away, he came hard enough that his knees buckled, and he ended up in a heap in the tub, water pouring over him.

A hard rap on the bathroom door brought him back to his senses fast. "Are you okay?"

"I'm fine, Mom," Aubrey called and tried to get back on his feet. "I slipped a little, but I didn't hurt anything."

"Are you sure?" The door handle rattled, and he was sure as hell glad he'd remembered to lock the door. "I can help you if you need it. Remember you ain't got nothing I haven't already seen." He could imagine her scolding stance outside the door.

"I'm fine," he repeated as he got to his feet, checking mentally that he hadn't broken anything. He hoped like hell he wouldn't have any bruises. Nothing looked worse under the club lights, and he'd have to try to cover them with makeup. He pushed back the curtain. "Could you make me some lunch?" He knew he had to give her something to occupy her mind, or she'd fixate on him.

"All right," she called, and Aubrey managed to finish his shower in peace and without falling out of the tub.

Once he was done, he dried off and dressed in light clothes. It felt good to just relax for a while. Sundays were the one day of the week that he tried to take it easy. His mom and dad had most likely gone to church that morning. Once he was presentable, he found his mom in the kitchen putting things on the table.

"I made cold things. It's too hot to cook, I hope that's all right."

He leaned down to her five-foot frame and lightly kissed her cheek. "Of course it is. Actually, it sounds delicious." She began setting places, one more than he thought necessary. "There's just the three of us."

"Margaret Lamston said that she and the deacon were going to be out of town for the afternoon, so she asked if we'd mind having Garrett over for lunch. It seems they spend Sunday afternoons together, and apparently he's some sort of hazard in the kitchen. Since you and he were such good friends, I knew you wouldn't mind."

Aubrey blinked. "Does Garrett know about this?" He hadn't seemed to when they were on their way home.

"Margaret said she called him a while ago and explained things."

Lord save them all from meddling mothers. Sometimes it was a wonder any of their sons grew up or left home without them right behind to push. "Of course it's okay. I saw Garrett in Dallas and brought him back with me. He didn't seem to know anything about it an hour ago."

His mother went about what she was doing, completely unconcerned, and sure enough, ten minutes later the bell rang, and his father came in the kitchen with Garrett in tow. It seemed the mothers' network was as efficient as it ever was.

"I'm sorry if my mother put you out," Garrett said as he came in. "She can be a little forceful."

Aubrey's mother snickered softly. "Your momma is a freight train going at full speed. God bless her."

"She's a force, ma'am, I can't argue with that." Garrett glanced his way, and Aubrey saw the truth mixed with a touch of fear. Garrett's mother had always given him a case of the worries as a kid. That woman always seemed to know what they were up to, and dang if she didn't have eyes in the back of her head. Not that his mother wasn't the same, but no one could sit you down, smile, and talk as sweet to you while making you feel as though you were going straight to hell for taking a single puff on a nasty cigarette or peeking around to see what the bulls were actually doing at breeding time. "She knows the way things should be, and that's just about that."

"Well, I reckon your momma knows what's right for a good Christian woman," his mother agreed as she started placing dishes on the table. "She works hard and helps a lot of folks." The dishes clunked on the table a little harder than was necessary, which probably meant his mother was giving lip service to what she thought she should say as opposed to what she really felt.

Garrett shrugged. "Can I help with anything? I know you weren't planning on me for lunch, and contrary to what my mother thinks, I am able to feed myself."

"It's almost ready, and don't you worry about it for a second. It's nice to have company." His momma did love to entertain and feed folks. It was one of her gifts. She placed the last bowl on the table, which groaned under the weight.

"How many people were you expecting to feed?" his father teased as he sat down. "You always make enough for a family twice the size."

"It's hard to cook less when you're used to making food for growing kids." She motioned to Garrett, and

Aubrey took his usual place and passed the dishes around. Only his momma could make a lunch for a king out of half a dozen salads and such, though the green Jell-O salad with coconut and marshmallows was something to be avoided at all costs as far as he was concerned.

"Did I get you back in time?" Aubrey asked Garrett.

"Yeah. I helped the other guys with feeding and then came over here." He took some of the potato salad and passed the bowl, helping himself to the egg salad and then the ham salad as they came around, followed by the bread. "Today's the slow day, just like here, I suspect. We do what we have to and really start in again on Monday."

"It's the life of a rancher. Work like hell for six days, take part of the seventh day off for the Lord, and then go right back to work," his dad said. "Done it all my life." He sighed, and Aubrey wondered what it was for, but no explanation seemed forthcoming.

"Why don't you boys go into town this afternoon? They're having an ice cream social at the church at four. It's for unmarried people to get to know each other." His mother was as subtle as a charging bull.

Aubrey lowered his head, suddenly doubly interested in the food on his plate. Garrett, on the other hand, broke into a winning smile. "That's not a bad idea. We can finish the feeding and then go to the church." He turned from Aubrey's mom to him, that smile not fading for a second. "Too bad it's too far to ride."

Aubrey nearly choked on his fork at the expression on Garrett's face. For the briefest of seconds, his desire lay naked, and Aubrey was glad his legs were under the table and his lap was covered by a napkin. What the hell was Garrett playing at?

"Well, I suppose if you wanted to go for a ride, you could head out to the creek. I bet it's pretty low right now." She turned from Garrett to Aubrey. "Maybe check that it isn't going to go dry."

"The creek's spring-fed, so it never goes completely dry," Dad reminded her. "Though it sure would be nice if we got some rain. We get weeks of it, so much it dang near washes everything away, and then someone shuts off the tap, and we can't get a lick of the stuff for months." He looked to the ceiling. "Just a little bit now and then would be all right."

"Barney," his mother scolded. "He knows what he's doing."

"Sometimes I wonder," his dad muttered under his breath and went back to eating.

"I think checking out the creek's a good idea. It may not go dry, but in this heat…. At least the wells have plenty of water after all that rain, so we aren't in any real danger this year." Though a little rain would green things up again and save him some on feed. Stuff was getting mighty brittle, though that was expected in early summer. With ranching, things were either feast or famine, it seemed. Aubrey went back to eating, trying like hell not to watch Garrett all the time, so mostly he ended up staring at his plate.

When he was done, he took his dishes to the sink and bussed Garrett's when he was done, as well. "I'm going to head out to the barn." He needed to get out of here before his mother brought up the ice cream social again. He had no intention of going, and the best way to make sure she didn't meddle was to be gone for a while.

Garrett seemed to sense the same thing and pushed back his chair. "Thank you, ma'am, for an amazing lunch." He leaned down and whispered something that made Aubrey's mother grin. She slapped his arm lightly. "Go on," she said, coloring, and Garrett left the kitchen. He was still smiling as they left the house.

"What did you say to her?" Aubrey asked. "Because if you complimented her cooking, she'll probably adopt you. She's always looking for folks to feed."

"I told her that her lunch was better than at my mother's," Garrett said.

"That's done it," Aubrey said seriously, stopping midstride. "You realize if word gets out, you'll have started a feud that will last for a decade. Every church potluck will become a battleground. Who can bring the best dish and then get the most people to eat it? Remember Cindy March and Jacquie Harper? They went at it for years, and I understand it was all because Cindy's husband complimented Jacquie on her cherry pie."

"Yeah, maybe. But those women were nuts," Garrett said, and a split second later, that wicked grin was back. "We sure did eat good all that time, didn't we?"

Aubrey chuckled. "You're awful." He bumped Garrett's shoulder with his and then continued on to the barn. "Let's get saddled up, and we can ride out." He pointed out where everything was in case Garrett didn't remember, and then they got to work brushing and saddling Klondike and Marigold, then led them out into the yard, where they mounted and got going.

It was hot, so they took it easy, careful not to push the horses. "I wasn't expecting my mother to arrange things the way she did," Garrett said after they'd been quiet a spell.

"I know." Aubrey had been thinking, keenly aware of Garrett riding next to him and the way he looked, tall and straight in the saddle. The guys in the club sure loved him as the cowboy of their fantasies, but what Aubrey really wanted was a cowboy of his own, and he was finding it hard not to let his fantasies run away with him. Garrett pulled ahead of him, so Aubrey hung back, watching Garrett's legs as they gripped the horse and his tight jeans-clad cowboy butt as it slowly rocked to the cadence of his horse. Broad shoulders and back, tapering to a narrow waist—Garrett wasn't huge, but he was pretty much Aubrey's idea of physical cowboy perfection.

He continued watching until the tree line got closer, and then they plunged under it. The shade was magnificent. It wasn't much cooler in reality, but they were out of the sun, and that in itself made quite a difference.

The creek was just a shallow stream of water at the moment, but it gurgled and meandered its way in its bank. At one point there had been talk of damming it or some such thing, but that seemed kind of stupid to Aubrey and mighty selfish to the folks downstream. So the little brook ran peacefully in its bed as Aubrey got off Klondike and tied him up, letting him munch the grass while Garrett did the same with Marigold.

"Remember we used to go swimming just around that bend?" Garrett asked.

"Yeah," he breathed, and instantly he was back there, the two of them swinging off the old rope and dropping into the water, yelling and screaming like crazy people. "That was the first place I realized—" He wasn't sure he wanted to go there, but the words were already out. "You know what I mean."

"So it's hard for you to talk about too," Garrett said, joining him once his horse was secured. They seemed content to munch, so Aubrey led the way down to one of the old fallen logs, where they both took a seat.

"Yes. I used to think there was something wrong with me. Everyone said having these feelings was wrong. I heard it in church… in school… you know. I used to go to the library and sit in the corner with the computer that faced away from everyone. That was before they got the filter program, and then I gave up."

"Were you looking at pictures?" Garrett asked. "Because I used to sometimes. But I was so afraid of getting caught and what would happen…."

"I know. Actually, there were some movies that I stumbled on. They were older, but they showed people like me. I almost got caught once, and then after that, I didn't go back for a while. When I did, the sites were blocked." Aubrey shrugged. "It felt like some friends had been taken away." He lifted his gaze to the sparkling ribbon of water.

"I never had that." Garrett turned to look at him at the same time that Aubrey did. Their gazes seemed to cross and then focus on each other. "You know my mom and dad. They would never understand, I know that. Mom is so self-righteous most of the time, and Dad lives in his own little world that's totally dominated by the church and his position in it. He'd never accept anything that would threaten that, and having a gay son would certainly not put him in a favorable light with the Bible crowd." Garrett sighed. "Your mother is pretty awesome, but even she was talking about all that at lunch and trying to get us to go to the social so we could pick out wives or something."

"Mom gets that idea in her head every now and then, but I'd never do that. I go sometimes, keep to myself, and all the girls just think I'm shy. Either that, or they have the idea that I'm simple. A few have tried pursuing me, but thankfully none of them have tried hard enough for me to really have to put them off. Mostly they see someone who works all the time and has to help take care of his parents. They don't want that."

"I suppose not," Garrett said. "Let's wander down and look at the swimming hole."

"It's gone," Aubrey said. "A couple years ago there was a storm, and enough water came down the creek that it changed course slightly. The hole filled in when some of the bank collapsed. I took down the rope so no one would try to use it." It had been like losing part of his childhood.

"That's a shame."

"Yeah, it is," Aubrey agreed, but what's gone was gone, and he couldn't bring it back. "But things change, and we grow up."

Garrett's gaze heated slightly. "You sure did." He knocked Aubrey's shoulder. "It would have been nice if we'd have known about each other, you know."

Aubrey shook his head. "Neither of us could keep our mouths shut then, just like everyone else. Besides, if I had told you, would you have opened up or just kept quiet about yourself? I know I wouldn't have said anything. I wasn't ready for anyone to know."

Garrett nodded. "I'm not sure I'm ready now." He paused for a moment, then said, "It's the shits, you know. We work hard all day and live our lives outdoors. We lift and tote things that would break most guys' backs. We're not weak men… and yet something like this leaves me about ready to throw up." He leaned back. "Am I completely stupid?"

"No. We have to live and work here. Standing up and saying who we are would mean your mom and dad would most likely never speak to you again, and who knows what would happen to the ranch if people stopped doing business with me. Mom and Dad can't keep it going by themselves. I'm as stuck as you are. I want to keep the ranch and live there for the rest of my life. It's my home. I don't want to devastate my parents, but I keep thinking that my mom has to know on some level that I'm never going to get married. I don't think she wants to admit it to herself."

The only time he didn't feel alone was when he was at the club, and even then he tended to keep himself separate from the other guys. They were all gay— at least, he thought so. He had never given it much thought, but it was possible some of the guys weren't and only did it for the money. They certainly weren't all like Simon, who spent as much time out back as he did on the stage.

"Sometimes life fucking sucks," Garrett said.

"Have you thought about moving away? There are places, lots of them all over the country, where being gay isn't such a huge deal. You could go and have a good life, find someone to share it with, and leave all this closed-minded shit behind." The temptation had most definitely been there for him, but he couldn't leave his parents alone with the ranch, not after his sister had scurried out of town as soon as she was old enough.

"I guess," Garrett said. "But what would I do somewhere else? This is all I know."

Aubrey scoffed. "Tell me about it." He had to pause and think about what he was going to say. "At least when I go to Dallas, people understand I'm from Texas and a cowboy. But I lived in Baltimore for a few months right after I washed out of college. I didn't start until late and ended up finishing early, and not in a good way." He'd enjoyed college life in Austin—too much, obviously, given his grades. He wasn't invited back after his sophomore year. God, that had been a shitty, tough time. "I had a lead on a good job. They needed someone who was willing to work hard. I was no stranger to that, so I signed on to work at the docks."

"Was it bad?"

"No. I could do the work, but it was more of the same. I thought I could be myself when I was there. But the other guys were just like the people here—closed-minded. I didn't fit in with anyone and ended up going out drinking all the time to forget how unhappy I was, and then I drank because nothing felt like home. Finally I was drinking to drink, and I woke up one day looking like hammered shit and decided I needed to go home." He picked at the tall scraggly blades of grass between his legs.

"Jesus," Garrett breathed.

"Yeah. But I'd drunk up all my money, so I worked another three months, stayed out of the bars, and kept to myself. Then I was making really good money, so I stayed three more months, until it got so cold I thought my balls were going to freeze off. Hard work I can do, but cold and wet that goes clear through to your bones…." He put up his hands in surrender. "I got me a bus ticket, pulled out all my money, quit the job, and got the hell out of town and home in time for Christmas last year."

Garrett smiled once again, but it seemed forced. "I bet your mom was thrilled."

"Yeah, she was. Went apeshit all over the place. She insisted I go shopping with her for Christmas." He dropped the grass he'd been playing with. "We were shopping, and one of Momma's credit cards was declined. She paid with another, but by then I'd figured something had to be wrong, so I made Daddy show me the books. They were really bad, so I used the money I had to stave off the wolves, made Daddy cut up their cards, and I've been up to my ears in work ever since." He let loose a breath until his shoulders ached. He hadn't even realized how much he'd been holding in until he let some of it go. He felt like a clock that had been wound too tight, and now some of that pressure was gone. He slumped forward and hoped to hell he didn't retch. He'd done so many things since the day he'd found out just how close they were to losing everything. He kept reminding himself he was doing what he had to so the ranch and his family could survive, dignity and pride be damned.

"Are things still bad?" Garrett asked.

Aubrey shook his head. "I let go of the land that wasn't productive for us anymore. That cut some expenses, and I sold off a number of things that we weren't using any longer."

"I heard you sold off some of the horses."

Aubrey nodded. "Damn near killed me to do it. But they brought in good money, and they cost money to feed. Daddy and Momma were angry with me for a week and didn't speak to me for two days… not one word. But they knew it had to be done. I used some of the money to pay down the debts and the rest to buy some more head that will bring in money down the road. It's hell being a small business, but I think, or at least I hope and pray, that we're on the right track now, 'cause if we're not, I don't know what more I can do except head off Daddy's buying more of what we don't need."

"It was no problem, and Bridger was giving your dad a break because they're friends, so I could give him a better price. Everybody came out ahead."

"Well, I'll remember what you did."

Garrett leaned a little closer. "I hope you'll remember this." He closed the distance between them until their lips touched and then sealed over each other. Aubrey closed his eyes and let the heat that out-sizzled the Texas summer run through him. Garrett kept it gentle until Aubrey leaned in, deepening the kiss and adding his own heat until they were both moaning softly. Damn, that was hot, and it left them both breathless and staring at each other, wide-eyed. Aubrey would have laughed, but he was too excited. When Garrett pounced on him, they both ended up falling off the log and onto their backs in the grass.

Garrett climbed on top of him, spreading his legs, working at one of Aubrey's shirt buttons with one hand until he could slip it inside and along Aubrey's skin. He'd been sweating up a storm, but Garrett didn't seem to mind. Hell, as soon as he broke the kiss, he was licking and sucking at his neck. "Jesus Christ," Aubrey swore and grabbed Garrett's hard, tight ass, pushing them together as he slowly rocked back and forth.

"Holy hell," Garrett whispered and thrust harder and faster.

"You need to stop, or we're both going to have squishy pants," Aubrey managed to warn between his gritted teeth. He wanted to yell and yank Garrett's clothes off so he could take him right here, deep and hard. He wanted that cowboy ass around him, tight heat gripping him. It was what he'd fantasized about for years.

"Aubrey!" he heard floating on the wind. Damn, his mom's voice would carry to Dallas if the wind was right.

He stilled, swearing under his breath, and tried to clear his head from the cloud of lust that had overtaken him.

"I heard her too." Garrett sat up slowly.

"I swear she knows whenever I'm doing something she doesn't approve of." Aubrey looked around, then stood up and retreated deeper into the woods, Garrett following. Once the limbs closed around them, Aubrey tugged Garrett to him, kissing him hard, possessively. When he heard his mother's voice on the breeze once again, he groaned and moved away. "I better get back before she has a conniption."

"Do you think something's wrong?" Garrett asked, gripping his arms tightly.

"I hope not." He really had no idea why she would be calling for him, but they walked to where they'd left the horses, mounted, and began the trip back to the house, going much faster than they had on the trip out.

"What's the problem?" he asked his mother as he reined Klondike to a stop in the yard.

"It's almost three. You need to clean up if you're going to go to that social."

Aubrey lifted his head to the sky. "Did it ever occur to you that I was happy, and that we were enjoying our quiet afternoon?"

"It's important that you go," she explained. "You've been working too hard, and you need to meet someone who can be a partner to you for the rest of your life, so when your father and I are gone, you won't be alone." She seemed urgent in her fervor.

"Mom, you and Dad are going to be around for a long time. And I'm too busy for things like that right now." He didn't want to bring up how hard he was working to get the ranch back on an even footing. He saw the determination in his mother's eyes dim just enough to know she understood what he wasn't saying.

"You can't work all the time, and you need to have some friends. Lady friends," she clarified when Aubrey turned to Garrett. "This is important."

"No, Mom. The ranch is important, and so are you and Dad. There's plenty of time for me to find someone." He crossed his arms over his chest. "Those socials attract a bunch of gossips, anyway, and you know it. If I want to meet someone, I'm perfectly capable to doing it on my own, in my own time."

She stepped forward. "Nonsense. Now, I know what's good for you, and I'm not backing down. So you march inside and get cleaned up so you will look presentable." She turned her fire-filled eyes on Garrett. "You too." She looked him over. "You can borrow some clothes from Aubrey. I just did laundry, and there's plenty of clean things in his room."

"We have to get the horses brushed and watered."

"Then get a move on," she snapped. "Your father is resting, so I need you to take me." She glared, and Aubrey knew he wasn't going to get anywhere with her. "Get the horses settled."

"Yes, Mother," he groaned and led his horse toward the barn.

Garrett followed behind and got his horse back in the stable and his saddle off. Then he brushed him down and made sure all the horses were fed and watered. By the time Aubrey was done, Garrett had stepped out of the stall, and they walked to the house together.

"You don't have to stay if you don't want to," Aubrey said. "In fact, it's probably best if you make a run for it now, before my mother gets her hands into you."

"Are you kidding? All the women at these things have baked and cooked for hours to make the food." His eyes filled with glee. "Just think about it. All you have to do is compliment each dessert as you eat it, and every mother and grandmother in the place will swarm all over you." He leaned closer as if sharing a secret. "Their daughters will never get close enough to see you because the mothers will be swarming like flies."

Aubrey rolled his eyes, and they went inside together.

He got Garrett some clean clothes and let him use the bathroom first. When Garrett came out dressed, Aubrey took his turn, tingling all over from their kiss and from the fact that Garrett was just outside his door. He showered for the second time and then pulled on a pair of fresh jeans and a light shirt. After checking himself in the mirror, he opened the door.

Garrett turned from where he'd been studying the things on top of Aubrey's dresser. Aubrey knew the minute Garrett saw him. His mouth opened slightly and his eyes bugged. "Jesus. I better rethink the plan I told you. No one in that room is going to leave you alone."

Aubrey looked down at himself. "What?"

"Please. You're a cowboy lover's wet dream."

"I am not."

"Haven't you ever looked at yourself in a mirror? You could be the cover model for one of those romance novels my mother reads." Garrett glided closer. "I mean it. You're one hot guy."

"Okay." He smiled. Garrett thought he was hot. For some reason that made him happier than all the yells, catcalls, and money that got thrown his way in the club. "Uh, thanks." He gave Garrett a leer so he could know that Aubrey thought he was hot too.

"I'm ready to go," his mother called impatiently. "I don't want to be late, or everyone will fill up on

Evelyn's lemon cake rather than my chocolate one."
Aubrey didn't try to understand the rivalries between
the hospitality committee members.

"We're ready," he called and stepped away from
Garrett, taking a deep cleansing breath and opening the
door. *Ready to walk into battle.*

Chapter Five

THE church auxiliary hall was full of people, with more arriving, as Aubrey carried his mother's cake and Garrett let her hold his arm. Aubrey had to admit she was beaming at the attention, and Garrett seemed to be doing his best to charm her. They'd known each other for most of his life. As he watched, Aubrey wondered if his mother might be lonely. Maybe that was why she'd taken to doing all that shopping. As far as he knew, she'd never been a spendthrift, but maybe something had changed.

"Is there something on my dress?" his mom asked, and Aubrey realized he'd been staring.

"No, Mom. You look pretty." He covered for his ruminations as they passed through the door and entered the fray. The overlapping conversations nearly knocked him on his butt. There was another reason he hated these things: the wall of sound was almost too much. The club was louder, but there he had a job to do and something to concentrate on. Here he felt like he was the center of attention, and not in a good way at all.

"I'm going to take care of my cake," his mom said. "You two sidle on over there to where Carrie and Bronwen are waiting. They've been asking after you." She fixed him with a hard stare, and Aubrey rolled his eyes. "I know you don't want me to do all the work for you, but I will if I have to."

"Now, Mrs. Klein, don't you worry. Aubrey and I will be good." Garrett looked over at the girls and flashed them a smile. Neither of them responded, and Aubrey got the feeling his mother was exaggerating just a little. Still, with her watching, Aubrey walked over and sat down at their table. He never knew what to say to girls. He really didn't understand them at all. He didn't want to lead them on.

"So what goodies did you bring?" Garrett asked. "I'm hungry, and I want to be sure to start with the good stuff." Sure enough, Carrie's formidable mother, Evelyn Parker, swooped in.

"Then you want the blueberry cobbler."

"And some of the lemon cake," another woman piped up, and they were off. Aubrey stared in amazement as plates were filled and brought back, set down in front of them as though they were their pride and joy.

"I heard you were working out East," Carrie said to Aubrey.

Aubrey held his fork still to answer her. "Yeah, I was working on the docks in Baltimore." He shrugged.

Carrie leaned closer. "Don't tell anyone, but I'm fixing to get out of here. This town is stifling, and I want to do more." She peered around. "I haven't told Momma yet, but I want to go to Philadelphia or someplace like that."

"You're going to freeze during the winter," Aubrey warned. "I never experienced cold like up there."

"You wanna see cold? Try telling your mother that you're never going to get married and give her grandchildren because you aren't interested in men." Carrie's eyes were hard as steel and serious as a cyclone. "I'm hoping to find somewhere I can meet some other women."

Garrett must have heard what she said because he nearly dropped his fork. Aubrey simply nodded. "Well, good for you." Now it was Carrie's turn to stare, and Aubrey grinned. She'd always been a spitfire in school, and while they knew each other, it was only on the periphery. "I think you deserve to be happy, no matter what. So more power to you."

"You ain't shocked? Momma nearly had a cow."

Aubrey laughed. "Honey, if you want to spend the rest of your life with another woman, I wish you every happiness, and if you're trying to shock me, you're going to have to work harder than that." He winked, and Carrie rolled her head back, laughing heartily. Aubrey realized he liked her even more. "But you don't have to leave. Just get online or something, find yourself a cowgirl, and ride off into the sunset."

Carrie's mother, of the famous blueberry cobbler, approached under a head of steam. She was a force to be reckoned with. "Are you talking about those… filthy things?" she whispered menacingly. "In the house of the Lord?" She turned to him. "I hope she didn't shock you."

"Not for a second," Aubrey said with a grin. "I think she should live her life the way she wants, and you should love your daughter for who she is." He was getting a little hot under the collar, and his patience was wearing thin with the intolerance he saw at every turn. Some music started through the loud speaker. "You line dance, don't you?" he said to Carrie.

"Of course," Carrie said, and she and Aubrey stood and moved to the center of the room. Some others joined them, and soon he and Carrie were kicking up their heels, boot scooting and toe tapping their way around the room. "Dang, you're really good. I wish I'd have known you could dance in high school."

The music changed to a two-step. "You game?" he asked.

"Hell, yes."

He took her hands and led her around the floor.

"I should have gone to the prom with you," Carrie said. "Billy Haskins had two left feet, and after an hour he tried to dance me out the door and under the bleachers."

"Did he succeed?" Aubrey asked.

"In getting a good case of knee in the balls, oh yes." She howled with laughter, and Aubrey joined in. It had been a long time since he'd had this much fun at a church social. "I think someone is looking at you." She tilted her head toward Garrett, and Aubrey did his best not to misstep.

"We're just friends," Aubrey said, toeing the line.

"Honey, if that's what you want to call it, okay, but fucking hell, if a girl looked at me the way he looked at you for those two seconds, I'd be out of here and trying to find somewhere private faster than you can say 'pussy tickler.'" Aubrey stumbled at that, and

Carrie snickered. "It's okay. I'm not going to spread it around to anyone."

"Thanks," Aubrey said, and just like that, he'd outed himself. Granted, it was only to Carrie, but he'd told someone in a roundabout way. He expected the world to come to an end, but it didn't. The music went on, and Garrett walked Bronwen to the floor. They danced, but they didn't really seem to be getting along, and Aubrey saw Garrett look over at him every few seconds. "Sometimes, at moments like these, I wonder if the entire building would come crashing down around us if Garrett and I did dance together."

"I think they'd have to call every ambulance in town because half the women and most of the men would have either strokes or heart attacks. The rest would set off on some self-righteous crusade." She leaned closer. "It just might be worth it, though." The song ended, and everyone clapped and then found their seats again.

Aubrey's plate was where he left it, and he went back to eating. "How long do these things last?" Aubrey asked Garrett, who'd sat down next to him.

"Till about six, I'd guess. Then everybody has to go for supper."

Aubrey looked at his plate and dug in again. Eventually, once he'd had more than enough, he took care of his plate. As he headed back to the table, his mother waylaid him. "I saw you dancing with Carrie. She's a little wild, but she knows ranching and was raised around cattle and horses."

"Mom. I'm not auditioning for a wife, and there isn't some set of boxes that you get to tick off to chronicle my journey from introduction to the altar." He checked his watch. "I did what you asked, and against the odds, I had a good time. Now I'm going to go home because I have some chores to do, and the livestock need to be fed and watered." He checked the weather radar on his phone and saw a line of heavy rain heading their way. He hoped it held together. Of course, if it did, they could be in for quite a blow.

"Everything all right?" Garrett asked.

"Looks like some weather heading our way." That was a good enough excuse for him to leave. "You had enough cake and mothering?" Aubrey teased, and Garrett nodded. "Then, Momma, we need to see about going. I don't want Daddy to try to tie everything down on his own."

"All right." She stiffened and began making the rounds to say good-bye.

Aubrey said good-bye to Bronwen and Carrie, telling the latter to come out for a visit sometime. Once they were all ready, he led the way out to the truck. "Do you need us to drop you off on the way?" he asked Garrett. The skies were already darkening as they sped away from town.

"Just take me to your place. I'm going to need my truck. They haven't issued any warnings or anything, so this might be one of those rainstorms without all the wind and such."

He hoped so. The last thing they needed was damage to the ranch that would require more money to fix. Aubrey sped up and pulled into the ranch. No drops had hit yet, but it was only a matter of time. His mom went right into the house, and Aubrey hightailed it for the barn with Garrett right behind him.

"I'll close the back doors," Garrett called, already hurrying as huge drops pinged against the windows. Aubrey called the horses that were outside, and they came inside in a hurry. The wind came up, blowing through the barn, then cutting off as Garrett yanked the door closed. "Looks like we're all getting what we need," Garrett yelled over the din of the rain on the roof.

"It sure does. I hope it doesn't flood like it did in the spring, but one of these each week sure would be welcome." The storms usually didn't last long, and by the time Aubrey had all the horses settled in their stalls, the rain was already letting up, and the skies were lightening.

He closed the last stall door and stepped into the center of the barn. Instantly, Garrett pulled him down the aisle and then pressed him against the stall wall, kissing and pressing to him. Fuck, that felt good, and he pressed back, grinding his hips to Garrett's, cock instantly hard and all his blood running south.

"Damn, you taste good," Garrett whispered, licking at his neck.

"Don't leave a mark," he groaned. That would be hard to explain and set his mother off on a quest to find out what he'd been up to.

"Everything okay?" his dad said from outside the barn.

Aubrey groaned, and Garrett backed away with a huff. "It's fine, Dad," Aubrey called, hoping his voice sounded normal as he made sure his clothes looked okay. "The horses are all watered and fed. I'll leave them in the barn for the night." He stepped around the stall and checked the door.

"Good." His dad looked around and then turned leave. "I thought I'd go have a beer."

"Okay," Aubrey said, his heart still pounding in his ears. "Have a good time and be careful driving." His dad waved and closed the barn door. Aubrey's breathing returned to normal, and Garrett joined him.

"I better be going. There will be things I need to do before morning."

Aubrey nodded and looked to the door once again. He thought about trying for another kiss, but with his luck, his mother would choose that moment to check on him, so he nodded and walked Garrett out, said good-bye, and then stood on the porch as Garrett turned around and drove off. It had been one hell of a weekend, he thought, and once Garrett's taillights disappeared, he went inside.

Chapter Six

"**MOM,** I'm heading out to Dallas," Aubrey called. "I'll see you tomorrow afternoon." It had been two weeks with no catastrophes or unexpected expenses, which was a miracle in itself. "Don't forget that Garrett is joining us for dinner."

"I remember," she told him from the kitchen.

"All the stock has been well watered and fed. They should all be just fine until tonight."

"Thanks, son," his dad said. "Helen, are you cooking already?"

She came into the room, wiping her hands. "Not yet. Are you hungry?"

"Nope. But with the young'un gone, I thought we'd go into town for dinner. You deserve a night out."

His mother seemed surprised. "Are you feeling okay?" She made a show of feeling his forehead.

"Yes. I'm tired of being tired and moping around. So we're going to go into town, have dinner, maybe do a little dancing at the supper club." He smiled, and Aubrey left the house to give them their time alone.

He hurried to his truck, threw his small bag inside, and pulled away. Last week he'd arranged with Barry to have his costumes cleaned so he wouldn't have to bring them home and manage to do a load of laundry without his mother knowing. Lord, that kind of stuff got old fast.

Garrett had asked about coming with him, but for the past two weeks, he'd had to work on Saturday, so that had bought Aubrey a reprieve. He wasn't sure what he was going to tell him when he finally had the chance to come along. He didn't want Garrett, or anyone else, to know what he was doing. If things kept up the way they had for the past few weeks, it looked like he'd be able to leave this part of his life behind in a month or so, and that would be awesome. He'd have the bills paid and the ranch on a solid footing, and the part of his life that he wasn't proud of would be behind him. Then he could start a proper life of some sort. Hopefully with Garrett.

The way to Dallas was so familiar he swore he could make the trip in his sleep. Traffic was light, and he arrived earlier than he intended, so he checked into the hotel and found a café around the corner. Like he always did, he kept a lookout for anyone familiar but saw no one. He ate quietly, keeping to himself, and then, when he was sure it was safe, he got into his truck and drove to his usual parking spot near the club. After checking one last time, he put on his mask and hat before jogging over to the club and going in the back door.

"I'll never understand how you can wear that thing in this heat," Simon said, walking around in nothing but a thong.

"Get dressed," Aubrey teased and slapped Simon's ass, the sound ringing off the walls. "Or at least what passes for dressed in this place."

"Dang," Simon whined, grabbing his cheeks. "You're stronger than you look." He moved closer. "You know, I really like strong guys, and…."

"No, thanks." Aubrey moved away. "You know it's not a good idea to get involved with the guys you work with. Leads to a real mess." Not that working at the club was like any job he'd had before and hadn't led to multiple complications already, but Simon was one he definitely didn't need.

"Are you sure?" He waggled his eyebrows.

"Yeah, I'm sure." He smiled and hoped this was one of those no-harm, no-foul situations. "Barry and the rest of the guys will be here soon, so we should get that routine we talked about last week down pat." Barry had asked them to do a double as a bonus spot, and that would certainly lead to more money for both of them, but only if it was good.

"We talked about the fireman thing," Simon explained, and Aubrey shook his head.

"Are you game to drive them wild?" Aubrey asked, and Simon nodded. "Then you come in on all fours like a horse with me riding you. I can put you in a pair of chaps and a jockstrap. They'll be throwing money." That was all this was about for him right now. The sooner he could make what he needed to clear the debts, the sooner he could quit and maybe start building a better life.

"Are you serious?"

"Yeah. I'm not that heavy, and all you need to do is get me to the center of the stage, then we can break into a routine to western music."

"If you think so." Simon seemed skeptical, but he went along with Aubrey's suggestion. They worked out a fairly simple routine in an hour and ran through it a few times to be sure. By the time they were done, Simon seemed convinced, and they took a break to leave the stage free for any of the other guys who needed to use it.

Aubrey got a little something to drink and waited for Barry's pep talk. Then he got dressed and ready for one of his routines. His nerves crackled, and he kept checking the crowd. He'd done that for three weeks, ever since Garrett had shown up that one time. Aubrey hadn't seen him since, but he kept looking. Finally it was his turn to go on, and everything went great. He made a ton and seemed to have the crowd in his hands. After he raced backstage, he changed into a different outfit and waited for Simon.

As their introduction began, Simon got down on all fours, and Aubrey stood over him. One of the guys shoved a riding crop into his hand, and he and Simon prepared to go for it. When it was time to go on, he held some of his weight and rode Simon onto the stage. The crowd went wild, and as soon as they reached the center of the stage, Aubrey turned and ended up staring right into Garrett's eyes.

He was supposed to stand up, but his legs seemed like noodles for a few seconds. Aubrey reminded himself that Garrett didn't know who he was, or at least he hoped to hell he didn't.

"Hey," Simon grunted.

Aubrey jumped off him, and they went through their routine. He collected his money, letting Simon handle the side of the club where Garrett had been standing, and as soon as he could, he hurried backstage.

"What the hell happened?" Simon demanded as soon as he joined him and began unloading the money they'd collected. Aubrey added his to the pile, and they began dividing it up. Aubrey didn't answer, and the other men went about their business because the show was continuing. "Was it someone in the audience?"

Aubrey's throat was still dry, and he nodded, swallowing hard.

"I get it. Do you think he recognized you?"

"Not this time, but if we're intimate, then I'm pretty sure he'll figure things out."

"Is this guy your boyfriend or something?" Simon took his half of the money and put it aside before peeling off his jockstrap and dressing for his next number.

"I don't know what he is. We've been friends for years, and we discovered things about each other recently. We've been spending time together, and I like him, but I can't get serious, really serious, with him as long as I'm doing this." He pulled at the thong he was wearing and let it snap back.

"You know, we aren't doing anything wrong. We provide entertainment. That's all." Simon had the decency to look sheepish. "You know what I mean."

"I've been telling myself that for as long as I've been here, and I nearly had myself convinced. But then I started to see him coming here, and…." Aubrey sat in one of the chairs and put his head between his legs.

"I need the fucking money for my parents. I thought that as long as my goals were noble, then I could keep doing this."

Simon laid his hand on Aubrey's shoulder. "If this is causing some sort of crisis for you, then walk away." When Aubrey lifted his gaze, Simon was fanning himself with a wad of bills.

"Bastard," Aubrey groaned. He just needed a month more. Why in the hell couldn't Garrett have stayed away from the place for a few more weeks?

"If you're so worried about him, just ask Barry not to let him in. Make up some story, and then you won't have to worry about it. After all, this guy, who you supposedly like, is spending his time in strip clubs." Simon raised his eyebrows. "Not that I'm saying there's anything wrong with it. Half our patrons are couples. They watch us and then go home and screw like rabbits."

"I don't have any hold on him, and we haven't made promises of fidelity or anything."

"Then what's the real problem? He doesn't know it's you. Talk to Barry and ask him to keep this guy out. You work as long as you need to and then say good-bye and go back to your life." Simon sounded jealous, and Aubrey wasn't sure he was being serious.

"It's not like that." Dammit, how could he explain to Simon that he had hopes that Garrett could be someone special? "I don't want to do this long-term. We're all in this for the money, and hopefully I can go back to the ranch."

"Do you want me to talk to Barry?"

"No. If he wants to come here, then I'm not going to take it away from him." There were precious few places where guys like them could go and have a good time without worrying about being harassed. "I'll just have to be careful." He had no other choice.

"Okay." Simon finished dressing, and Aubrey did the same. "We have the finale soon, and then we can rest a little before the second show."

Aubrey nodded and finished his costume change. When he went out on stage again for the finale, he didn't see Garrett, but he knew he was in the room somewhere—he could feel his gaze. When he left the stage, Aubrey kept to himself and out of sight. He didn't mingle with the crowd or go out back, where some of the guys went for their extracurricular fun. Instead, he stayed inside, got ready for the next show, and helped the bartenders refresh what needed to be replaced.

Thankfully, for the second show, he didn't see Garrett at all and was able to dance his numbers, collect his money, and get the hell out of there. It wasn't until he pulled into the hotel that he saw a very familiar truck parked in the center of the lot. Of course Garrett would stay at the same hotel he'd been using. After all, it was where he'd brought him. Aubrey stowed his mask in the glove compartment and got out, then hurried to his room. He'd gotten his key card out and was unlocking the door when he felt a gaze boring into the back of his head. "I was hoping to find you here."

"Were you following me?" Aubrey asked. "I was only out with some friends."

"I came down once my chores were done and had a few drinks." Aubrey knew Garrett was skirting the truth, but that was his business. "I like coming here sometimes. There are fewer eyes looking at me all the time."

"I know," Aubrey agreed and opened his room door.

Garrett looked around and then followed him inside, closing the door behind them.

Aubrey debated telling Garrett that it was late and he was dog tired, but the fatigue that had been settling in flew right out the window. The thought this might be a bad idea flitted around the back of his mind, but as soon as Garrett's lips found his, he forgot about everything else. He'd been denying himself for far too long. There was only so much teasing he could take, and having Garrett pressed to him, hot body quivering as badly as his, was too much to resist.

"Now," Garrett moaned.

"What?" Aubrey groaned, and Garrett crashed his lips into his once again. At a time like this, conversation was vastly overrated. He held Garrett tight, wanting no space between then. The grooves in the old room door bit into his back, but Aubrey paid it no mind.

His cock throbbed in his pants, straining for release. He had to think for a second and was thankful he'd been sweaty enough that after his last number he'd changed clothes completely. "Fuck," he groaned.

"Yeah," Garrett agreed, even though Aubrey had been swearing because at a moment like this the last thing he wanted intruding was the web of lies and deceit he'd built in his life.

"I need…." Aubrey moaned, and Garrett pulled him away from the door, propelling them both toward the bed. Aubrey fell back onto it, and Garrett yanked at his belt, pushing up his shirt, licking his belly while he fumbled with his pants. Aubrey held his breath as Garrett got his belt and pants undone, pulling the light fabric aside and stretching the waistband of his underwear until Aubrey's cock popped free.

He released his breath with a long groan as Garrett
took his cock between his lips. Aubrey closed his eyes,
running his fingers through Garrett's coarse hair. It felt
great in his hands, strong and rough, like a cowboy's.
"That's it," he breathed.

Garrett pulled away, and Aubrey opened his eyes,
meeting Garrett's heated gaze for a few seconds before
Garrett took him once again, plunging him halfway
to heaven. He and Garrett had been friends for years,
but this was so much better than that. A shiver went
through him when Garrett took him to the root, holding
him there while he stroked his hands under his shirt and
up his belly to his chest, plucking at his nipples until
Aubrey had trouble seeing straight.

"Garrett," he moaned and pushed his hips forward
to get that little bit more friction. When Garrett pulled
back once more, he left Aubrey panting on the bed.

"Get out of these," Garrett told him as he pulled at
Aubrey's shirt.

Aubrey kicked off his shoes and let Garrett yank off
his shirt. Garrett was in a definite hurry. Aubrey's pants
followed, and then Garrett jumped off the bed, shedding
his own clothes in frantic motions. Aubrey took those
precious few seconds to reach for the bedside light
switch, plunging the room into darkness.

More than anything he wanted to see Garrett, but
that would mean that Garrett would get a good look at
him naked, which meant he'd get a chance to compare
him to the Lone Rancher, and that wasn't a viable option.
He was playing a dangerous game, but he didn't want to
lose Garrett, and if things worked out as he planned, the
Lone Rancher would be history in a short time.

"You don't seem like the shy type," Garrett
observed, and Aubrey reached for him, pulling him

down onto the bed, wrapping his legs around Garrett's waist, luxuriating in the feel of Garrett's bare skin against his. Aubrey kissed Garrett hard, stroking his back, some parts of which were rough and others smooth and soft. Hard work, lifting, and constant cuts and abrasions often left cowboys rough and scarred. It was part of what he loved. Garrett's body, with its corded muscle that flexed beneath his hands, was the result of a life of hard work.

"I just want quiet, darkness, and you," Aubrey whispered. Garrett pulled away, hovering over him. Aubrey cupped Garrett's cheeks, holding them before guiding him down into a deep kiss.

"Are you sure?"

To answer him, Aubrey tightened his legs and thrust upward. Garrett got the message, stroking slowly along his thighs and down to his ass, exploring with excruciating slowness, leaving Aubrey breathless with anticipation. "Oh yeah."

"Do you have supplies?"

Aubrey hummed that he did, and Garrett rolled onto the mattress. Aubrey jumped off the bed and hurried to the bathroom. He ripped open his kit and got the condoms and a small bottle of lube, scattering some of the contents of his bag on the counter, but he didn't really care. Hurrying back to Garrett, he pressed the things into his hand. Then he stood next to the bed, watching Garrett's dark form come closer.

Garrett stroked his arm, enticing him closer with only the barest touch. "We have all night."

"Yeah."

"No mothers or socials, or any other interruptions." Garrett pressed his hand to Aubrey's chest, lightening the pressure, and Aubrey leaned closer, wanting more.

When his legs hit the bed, Garrett drew him down, enfolding him in his arms and holding him tightly. "For tonight, you're all mine."

Aubrey thought about that and realized he liked it. They were alone in their cocoon, and the rest of the world and all his fears and worries could be put on hold. He didn't have to worry about ranches, livestock, rain, or money for a few hours. He could put himself in Garrett's hands and leave it all to him.

"You're incredibly hot," Garrett whispered into his ear before sucking on it. Aubrey's eyes rolled around in his head, and he lolled his head onto the pillow, giving Garrett all the access he wanted.

"So are you," Aubrey breathed. "And I want to taste just how hot you are." He shook with excitement at the thought.

"Oh yeah." Garrett shifted onto the bed, and Aubrey changed places, using Garrett's body as a road map, sucking at his belly and then down to his cock as Garrett did the same. He thrilled at the sensation of Garrett sliding along his tongue as he sank between Garrett's lips, into wet heat that had his head swimming with passion. He shook his hips slightly, and Garrett mirrored his actions. Aubrey closed his eyes, pressing Garrett onto his back, straddling him.

Garrett's flavor, rich, salty, and scented with musk, burst onto his tongue. Aubrey loved it, but the combined sensation of surrounding Garrett while he was surrounded by Garrett nearly short-circuited his mind. Garrett stroked the backs of his thighs, parting his cheeks, adding more thrills, compounding excitement on top of passion. Just when Aubrey wasn't sure he could take any more, Garrett pushed him back and sat up.

Aubrey panted breathlessly and rolled over onto his back. Garrett pounced on top of him, parting Aubrey's legs. "I can't wait anymore," Garrett whispered as he shivered against him. "I want you so bad I can't stand it."

"Why?"

Garrett stilled completely. "What?"

"Why would you want me?"

"Fuck." Garrett breathed. "I spent my entire life waiting for someone like you, and hell, you were there the whole time. You know what my life is like because you've lived it, and you're an upstanding guy who doesn't play games. You're hot, and you've been there all along."

Aubrey knew he wasn't all those things. He'd been lying to Garrett and everyone else. "But—"

Garrett kissed him, silencing him. "You're everything I could possibly want and more." Garrett caressed down Aubrey's side and over his thighs. Without thinking, Aubrey raised his legs, and Garrett teased his entrance. Aubrey arched his back, rational thought once more slipping away as his mind clouded with desire.

The soft snick of a bottle opening reached his ears after Garrett's magic touch slipped away. He recognized it as the top of his bottle of lube. Then slick, magical fingers circled his entrance before slowly plunging inside him. The burn was magnificent, and as the sensation tore through him, he clung to Garrett with everything he had.

"Oh hell!" He couldn't stop the cry, throwing his head back.

"Good?"

"Magnificent."

"Then you're ready for me," Garrett said breathily.

"You better believe it." He quivered when Garrett pulled his fingers out. He felt Garrett pull away, knowing he was rolling on a condom, getting ready. Then Garrett leaned forward once again, and Aubrey grabbed him, holding him close as their bodies joined in the darkness. He groaned loud and long. The walls of this room were most likely paper thin, but he didn't care if he was serenading the people in the adjacent rooms. He wanted everyone to know how alive he felt with Garrett. So much of his life had been hiding and worrying about what other people thought of him. Right now, at this moment, the only person who mattered was Garrett, and each touch only showed him just what he had been missing from his life: someone who cared about him and wanted to make him feel as though he mattered.

Garrett entered him slowly, thick and hot, filling him incredibly.

"Damn," Garrett whimpered.

"You can say that again." Aubrey's head pounded with unabashed delight as Garrett seated deeper inside him. The connection was amazing, physical, and something deeper he couldn't put into words.

Then Garrett began to move. Aubrey continued holding on, pulling Garrett closer, until his breath ghosted over Aubrey's cheeks and lips.

"That's it," Garrett encouraged.

"What is?" Aubrey panted. Focusing on anything but what Garrett was doing to him proved difficult.

"That." Garrett pressed inside, hard. Aubrey held his breath for a few seconds and then released it. "Your breathing tells me everything about how you're feeling." He began moving faster, and Aubrey breathed in time to his movements, his head momentarily feeling light, swimming slightly, and then clearing. It was wonderful. All Aubrey did was concentrate on his own breathing, and Garrett seemed to read his mind, going faster and slower, even alternating his angle based on his reaction.

Within seconds, Aubrey was in heaven—touch, smell, taste, hearing, even his limited sight, all concentrating on Garrett, tuned to him. It was unlike anything he'd ever felt before.

"Stroke yourself," Garrett told him. "I want to feel you climax around me."

Aubrey did as he was told, already so close to the edge that he was going to come within seconds. Garrett held his sides, driving into him, rubbing that place inside, and Aubrey couldn't hang on any longer and tumbled over the edge, shaking as his release barreled through him, with Garrett following right behind.

Neither of them moved for a long time, joined together, holding one another, breathing softly. Aubrey was half afraid to move for fear Garrett would realize what they'd done and decide he wanted to leave.

Of course, as the haze of afterglow faded, his own doubts came racing back along with Garrett's words. Aubrey really did want to be the man Garrett thought he was, and that only hardened his determination to bring the secret part of his life to an end. A few weeks, a month at the most, and if the tips kept up, he could pay off the worst loan hanging over their heads and have the ranch on a footing where it could support itself and the family. That was what mattered. He'd managed to keep all the balls safely in the air this long; he could keep doing it for a little while more.

"Should I go back to my own room?"

Aubrey hummed softly and pulled Garrett a little closer. He didn't want him going anywhere, certainly not tonight. He was tired and needed to think. "Please stay."

"Okay," Garrett said. There hadn't been any words of undying devotion, but the way Garrett got up, cleaned him with the gentlest touch, and then climbed back into bed and held him as though he were the most precious thing in the world, told him a lot more than the words. For the sake of the ranch and his heart, he had to keep juggling those balls a little while longer.

Chapter Seven

"HOLY shit on a shingle," Aubrey said out loud.

"There'll be no talk like that in my house," his mother scolded from outside the office door with a basket of laundry in her hands. "That's—" She was about to start preaching, Aubrey could feel it. Sometimes he thought his momma should take over for the reverend.

"All right," he groaned and turned away from her. The last three weeks had been hell. He was dog tired, but the tips had been outstanding. And thankfully Garrett hadn't shown up again at the club, though the two of them had seen each other at least once a week for dinner and some time alone when they could manage it.

"Don't be short with me," she scolded, pulling Aubrey out of his daydream about the last time they'd ridden out to the creek. He bit his lower lip so hard he almost drew blood to stop the meanness that welled up.

"Maybe you deserve it," he whispered, and of course there was nothing wrong with her hearing.

The laundry basket hit the floor with a clap that rang off the walls. "What does that mean?"

Aubrey glared at her. He loved his momma, he really did, but there were times when she tried his patience and then went on to work his last nerve. "I just paid off the last of your credit card bills." He turned and met her gaze. "I wrote the check for the last one."

"So I can use them again," she said with a smile.

"No. I closed the accounts when I made the final payments. They're gone, and the ranch will pay no more of those bills."

"But…," she sputtered.

"He's right, Helen. From now on we pay cash for everything," his father said gently. "You and I nearly spent ourselves out of our home. Those cards and me not being able to concentrate on the work no more…. They were going to take everything." There was a light in his father's eyes that Aubrey hadn't seen in well over a year. "So we're clear?"

"We still have the mortgage on the ranch, which is sizable." But thankfully long-term. "We're current on all our other bills."

He and his father shared a long look, and Aubrey could almost feel the wheels turning in his head, but he didn't say anything, and Aubrey set his jaw to let his father know it was a subject that wasn't open for discussion.

His mother looked back and forth between them, then left the room, and Aubrey heard her pick up her basket.

After a few seconds, his father closed the office door. "You haven't been doing anything illegal, have you?"

Aubrey shook his head. "No, Dad. I haven't done anything illegal." That he could answer honestly. He wasn't sure about the morality of what he'd been doing, but that was beside the point. He needed to make sure that the family's future was secure.

"Okay. I'm going to trust that you're an adult and you know what you're doing." He didn't sound completely convinced. "But whatever it is that you've been doing, I want you to know we're grateful."

"I know you are, Dad," Aubrey said and closed the computer program that kept all of the ranch accounts.

"I'll take care of the evening feeding. Why don't you call that friend of yours and go have some fun. You've been working too hard." He took a step closer. "And don't think I haven't noticed that every time you go to Dallas to have some fun time with your 'friends' that you come back looking more tired than when you left."

Aubrey swallowed but said nothing and held his head still.

"Like I said, whatever it is that you're doing, your mother and I are grateful, and as long as you aren't doing anything illegal, we'll trust your judgment. Just don't think she and I don't see what's going on."

"Yes, sir," Aubrey said and waited for his father to leave the room before slumping back into the chair like a deflating balloon. He thanked all that was holy that his father hadn't asked exactly what he'd been doing, because he didn't think he'd have been able to lie directly to him. A few more weeks, and this whole chapter in his life would be over. He could hang up his mask and costumes and go back to just being a rancher. Just two more weeks, and he'd have enough to supplement the small nest egg so they'd have the money to enlarge the herd and give the ranch additional profit potential. After that, he had other plans to make the ranch even more self-sufficient.

Aubrey got up from his chair and patted his pockets for his phone. He remembered he'd set it on the desk, picked it up, and called Garrett. "Hey, it's me. I was wondering if you'd like to get a bite or something tonight."

"You aren't working?" Garrett asked.

"Dad said he'd feed tonight, so I figured I'd take advantage."

"You two should stop by the bowling alley," his mother said, sticking her head in. "Tonight is ladies' night, and the place will be filled with women. You could make an impression and maybe meet someone new."

Aubrey didn't respond to her.

"Your mom and my mom have been comparing notes," Garrett said. "She called to tell me the same thing not an hour ago."

"Lord save us from busybody Christian women," Aubrey said a little louder than he had to, and Garrett guffawed on the other end of the line. He heard his mother grumble as she continued on. "How about we play it by ear?"

"I like the sound of that," Garrett said softly. "I'll meet you at the steakhouse in an hour?"

"Perfect." Aubrey hung up and figured it was time to get cleaned up before his evening out.

AUBREY walked into the steakhouse and tried not to smile too big when he saw Garrett at one of the tables in front by the windows. He slid into the seat across from him. "What's got you so happy?"

"Just that things are going well at the ranch," Aubrey said. Having the financial monkey off his back was a huge relief.

Garrett leaned over the table. "Mr. Bridger told me today that his foreman—you know Jake Hammond— well, it seems that he's going to retire and move to be with his daughter and grandkids in Florida. He asked me if I'd like the job." Garrett was nearly bouncing in his seat. "It's a huge jump in responsibility, but it's what I want to do."

"Have you told your folks?" Aubrey asked.

Garrett shook his head. "They don't understand my interest in ranches and cattle. They think I should have gone to college. Of course, Dad wanted me to go to divinity school, but I'm not interested in any of that." Garrett looked around again.

"What's with you?" Aubrey asked.

"Nothing."

"You keep looking around."

"Haven't you noticed that our mothers have been spending a lot of time talking? They both suggested we go to the bowling alley, and last week they were pushing us to go to that Lonely Hearts dinner." Garrett shuddered, and Aubrey had to admit that whole idea gave him the willies. "I'm starting to think that half the town is spying for them. My mom knew I didn't go to that Lonely Hearts thing and was waiting for me at the front door."

Aubrey smiled. "Mine was too, but I refused to listen to her." He lowered his voice. "The way I see it, they seem to think we'll go to these places together, so…." He raised his eyebrows. "Maybe after dinner, we'll decide to bowl a game. We can always get a lane, have a good time, make an appearance, and then go somewhere much more interesting."

"So this whole thing with our mothers doesn't bother you?"

"This is a small town, and just about everyone knows your mother or my mother." Aubrey looked through the restaurant. "Just over there are Mr. and Mrs. Harten—they have the Circle H." Mrs. Harten turned and smiled at him. Aubrey nodded and smiled back. "I'm sure there are others in this place, so unless we want to tell them all the truth, then we have to put up with the meddling mommas."

"Lord, I'm not sure I'm ready for that."

"Hi, Garrett, Aubrey. You two ready to order?" Gayle asked. She'd been a year behind Aubrey in high school.

"I'd like a Dr Pepper and the T-bone special, medium, with the loaded baked potato and ranch dressing on the salad," Aubrey told her. Garrett ordered the same, but he wanted his steak medium rare.

"Sounds good," she said, looking at Aubrey a little longer than was necessary, and then she turned to Garrett. "Your mother was in here yesterday with one of her groups, and she said you were becoming social." Aubrey wanted to laugh at the awkwardness. "I was thinking that maybe we could go out sometime."

"That would be nice. But…." Garrett blinked a few times. "I thought you were dating Guy Peterson?"

Gayle shrugged. "Things have been a little off and on with him. Mostly off, lately."

"And you thought we could go out, maybe to a movie, have dinner here in town, make sure we were seen and that word would get back to Guy."

Gayle nodded slowly. "You aren't mad, are you? He says he loves me, but he seems so wishy-washy. For some kind of huge badass football player, he can't make a decision about anything."

"Honey, I'll go out with you and make sure you're seen all over town. We can make Guy so green with envy that he'll get down on his knees faster than a preacher in a crucifix warehouse."

Gayle's smile was brilliant. "You really will?"

"Sure. We'll have a good time."

"What if Guy decides to show up while you're on this date?" Aubrey asked.

"I can handle him. He just needs a push, and a handsome cowboy with me on his arm will be just the ticket." She turned and half bounced to the service computer.

"Well, you made her happy," Aubrey said, not knowing what he felt about this situation.

"Yeah, well, people will see me out on a date and suspicion will be allayed for a while. And my mother will get off my back. Heck, when Gayle goes back to Guy, I can act disappointed, and that should keep Mom at bay for at least a couple of months."

"Dang, you're devious," Aubrey told him with a sly grin. "Now if I can get my mom to leave me alone…."

"No worries. Just flirt a little with the various women at the bowling alley. Don't go too far, but be nice and smile a lot."

"But that's the problem. I don't want a girlfriend, and I'm not going to lead anyone on. We can go, and I'll be nice, but that's all." Gayle brought their drinks and salads, still all smiles. They ate, talked, and otherwise had a nice meal together. Gayle made sure their glasses stayed full and that they didn't want for anything.

She and Garrett set a date for the following Tuesday evening. Once both of them were full, they paid the bill and left the restaurant, walking through the twilight to the bowling alley. They found a free lane and set about bowling a game.

Sure enough, it didn't take long for some of the ladies to wander over and start conversations. To his surprise, Aubrey had a good time, and once their game was over and they'd each had a beer, they said good night to the ladies and made for the door.

As soon as Aubrey reached the door and stepped out into the night, the tension and pressure he'd felt all evening finally slipped away. He took a deep, cleansing breath and turned his head and gazed up past the neon sign to the dark sky pinpointed with a thousand tiny lights.

"You really are at a loss with women, aren't you?" Garrett said as they slowly made their way back to where they'd parked.

"Yeah," Aubrey answered but added no more. It didn't take long for them to reach the car, and Aubrey pulled open his door, wondering what they were going to do. He hoped this wasn't the end of the evening, but he wouldn't blame Garrett if it was. Aubrey felt drained. All night long, sitting and talking to the ladies, it was as if he was on display. They'd watched everything he did, and a few of them hung on every word. One woman he didn't know, someone's friend from out of town, actually leaned in and whispered that she'd never been with a cowboy and wondered if he'd be willing to take her back to her hotel and show her how to ride. Aubrey's mouth had gone dry.

Thankfully the friend had come to his rescue without knowing it. "She's drunk," she whispered and led the cowboy hunter away to get her some coffee. Still, Aubrey hadn't known how to react. He'd like to think most straight guys would have been gentlemanly, but he knew some would have taken advantage. All of them would probably have been turned on, but he'd simply sat back, stunned and aching to get the hell out of there.

"Why don't you leave your truck here and ride with me? I'll bring you back," Garrett offered.

Aubrey thought for about two seconds, watching Garrett in the lights in the parking lot, his breath hitching. He'd been watching him all evening in those damn tight jeans and shirt that hugged just the right places, outlining his chest every time he moved just right.

Aubrey pushed his door closed, locked the truck, and stepped around to Garrett's passenger door, trying like hell not to stare at him. That was damn hard… and so was he, as a matter of fact. Just watching Garrett got him revved up more than being on stage. He climbed in, and Garrett did the same, the overhead light turning off as soon as the doors were closed. "I know a great spot," Garrett said and put the truck in reverse, backing out of his parking spot before speeding them off into the night.

"I know this spot too," Aubrey said a few minutes later when Garrett pulled to a halt. "We camped here as kids." He got out. "I haven't been here in…." He looked at the view from the small hill. "It's pretty much the same."

"Yeah, it is," Garrett whispered, his voice drawing Aubrey to him like a moth to flame. "We used to pitch that old tent my dad had, and we'd stay out here, talking, telling each other stories and stuff." The tailgate of the truck banged as Garrett lowered it, and

Aubrey hoisted himself up, taking a seat. "It's like we were in another world."

Garrett sat down next to him. "Everything was so…."

"Simple and easy then. We were kids, and we talked about shit that didn't mean anything, but we thought we were unlocking the mysteries of the universe. I remember looking up at those stars and you telling me where Mars was and that you wanted to go there so you could be the first person ever to meet a real Martian." Aubrey bumped Garrett's shoulder. "I remember thinking how dumb you were because I knew there were no Martians. I'd seen that on TV. When I told you, you said I was wrong."

"Well, I was ten."

"Yeah. But you were still dumb," Aubrey teased, and thankfully Garrett chuckled. "I love your laugh, you know that?" Aubrey turned to him. "It's warm and kind." It wrapped around him in a way, but he didn't say anything like that to Garrett. Instead, he held still, watching him, or what he could see of him. There was enough light that when Garrett leaned closer, he was ready for it.

"I like your eyes, even though I can't see them right now. They remind me of the sky, that color when there isn't a cloud anywhere to be seen, bright and vibrant." He continued closer, and Aubrey stilled. Garrett gently slid his hands along his cheeks, and their lips met. Aubrey's eyes closed, and he slipped his arms around Garrett's waist, pulling them together.

"You know, you were the only friend I had back then, and you never disappointed me."

Aubrey smiled, Garrett's hot breath on his lips. They were so close. "What about that time I woke you up by putting frogs in your sleeping bag?"

"Okay. You slimed me a few times, but you never disappointed me. I always knew you'd be there for me. My mom and dad always wanted me to be what they wanted." Garrett shivered like he was cold, but Aubrey knew that wasn't possible. The night was way too warm. "They used to punish me by making me memorize Bible verses, and then they wondered why I didn't want to be a pastor. I got enough of all that as a kid." Garrett stilled.

"You told me about that." Aubrey knew because more than once he'd called, and Garrett's mom had said he was being punished. At least he'd usually been given extra chores and stuff.

"I never told you that's just what my mom used to do. My dad had a belt...."

Aubrey's hands automatically slid down Garrett's back to the marks he felt on Garrett's lower back. Garrett didn't have to make the connection for him; Aubrey knew now where they'd come from. "I was afraid it might be something like that."

"You knew?" The pain in Garrett's voice reached deep down, touching Aubrey's heart.

"I thought. People don't think kids see things, but we do. I didn't know why you hurt sometimes. I guess I thought you'd fallen." Now so many things made sense, like the times Garrett had barely been able to sit down in school. Aubrey released Garrett, his hands clenching into fists.

"Maybe we should go," Garrett said and slid off the tailgate.

Aubrey jumped to his feet, ready for a battle that would never come, the enemy of the moment too far out of reach. "Why?"

Garrett strode away toward the edge of the rise. "I never should have told you."

"Jesus," Aubrey said, his hands unclenching and his anger for his friend draining away, replaced by concern. "I wasn't mad at you. But I don't think I want to see your father anytime soon."

"It was a different time, and I should have known to leave well enough alone. That's what my mom says."

Aubrey approached Garrett's dark figure slowly. "Have you ever talked to your father about what he did?" He tentatively touched Garrett's shoulder. "You know his temper wasn't your fault."

"Well," Garrett huffed. "There must be something wrong with me." He turned. Aubrey's eyes must have adjusted to the darkness, because the fire and old, bone-deep hurt in Garrett's eyes was unmistakable, and it sent a chill running through him. "You jumped away as soon as I told you."

"Because I wanted to kill your father," Aubrey said, clenching his fists and holding them up. "I swear to God, and…." He waved them in the air, clenching his teeth. "I'd felt the scars, and I thought they were from work or something." He'd had cuts and hurts on and off his entire life; it came with the job.

"Oh."

Aubrey pulled Garrett to him.

"I was always such a disappointment to them. I was never good in school, and my dad is so smart. He wanted me to follow in his footsteps, and I… I wanted to be like your dad." Aubrey held him closer, wondering if Garrett was crying. "Then to top it off, I turn out to be something my father and mother will hate." He stepped back and stomped away.

Aubrey opened his mouth to offer advice, but he had none. Lord knew he didn't have any fucking answers. He kept who he was to himself, and when he did let the true part of himself out, at least his gay self, he wore a mask to try to hide who he was. "Sometimes life just sucks." That was the very best he could do and be truthful.

"No shit," Garrett breathed. "But like I said, you never disappointed me. You were always there, even if you didn't know why I was hurting."

"Well, yeah, I'm your friend."

Garrett turned to him. "I think you're a lot more than just my friend."

Aubrey's throat constricted, and he moved closer to Garrett once again. He was pretty sure he felt the same way, but the words got caught in his throat. Instead, he pulled Garrett into a kiss that curled his toes. He hadn't ever meant to fall for his friend. Hell, he figured they'd have some fun, maybe be a little less lonely, and then go back to being friends. He'd seen that with some of the dancers at the club. Sometimes they hooked up, and afterward, things went back to the way they'd been. Other times things hadn't turned out so well, and one of the guys left. Aubrey had figured his pull toward Garrett would fade over time and the intense attraction had been mostly because he'd kept to himself for so long. But maybe it was more than that. Shit, maybe this… thing… with Garrett was the real deal.

The thought both thrilled him and scared him half to death. He had never really thought he'd be able to find someone. He certainly knew he wasn't going to at the club, and having a boyfriend in Dallas wasn't going to work. His life was at the ranch, so he'd pretty much been prepared to spend his life alone.

"Are you okay?" Garrett asked.

Aubrey realized he'd been standing stock-still. "Yeah." He forced a smile. "I'm fine."

The fact that he hadn't told Garrett everything nagged at him, but after just a few more weeks, he'd be done at the club, that part of his life would be behind him, and he could move forward without that weekly blow to his pride.

Garrett kissed him again, and thoughts of dancing and even parents wielding belts flew from his head as Aubrey quivered with excitement. Nothing had ever felt as good as holding Garrett in his arms. Aubrey's jeans had become way too tight, and his cock pressed to the back of his zipper. He wanted Garrett so badly he couldn't think of anything else. He tightened his grip and lifted Garrett off his feet.

"Jesus…," Garrett swore breathily. Aubrey carried him to the truck and set him down on the tailgate before pushing him back with his lips and tongue.

"Hold on," Garrett said. Aubrey stilled, and Garrett shimmied away before hurrying to the cab, pulling the driver's door open. Aubrey blinked at the light, closing his eyes for a second. The door slammed closed and Garrett returned. The scent of horse reached his nose as Garrett spread a blanket on the truck bed. Then he covered it with a second lighter one. The intense scent faded as Garrett climbed in the bed, enticing Aubrey forward.

Aubrey followed as though Garrett were a huge red flower and he a hummingbird. There wasn't anything he could do to stop it. He wanted Garrett with everything he had, and nothing was going to stop him. He climbed up on the tailgate and prowled closer to Garrett, locking his gaze where he thought his was.

The heat in the warm night ratcheted up quickly. Aubrey felt the connection between them like a rope, and Garrett was the winch. When he reached his goal, he pressed Garrett back, lips just above Garrett's, eyes locked together. Aubrey didn't touch him, he only looked, letting his feelings come through, hoping it was clearer than his feeble words could manage. He parted his lips and saw Garrett follow suit. Then he lowered his lips to Garrett's and groaned when Garrett closed his arms around his neck. Aubrey pressed Garrett down, deepening the kiss as his legs and back shook with anticipation.

Aubrey felt Garrett smile against his lips. "Are you part dog or something?"

"No, smartass."

Garrett stilled, stroking his cheek. "I remember how you used to shake sometimes when you got excited. You did that when we were at camp and they were going to show us how to swim." Aubrey nodded. "You jumped in first."

"I could hardly stand still any longer and needed to get it over with."

"Is this like that? Something to get done?"

"No." Aubrey leaned closer, ghosting his lips above Garrett's. "This is something I want to last forever and don't want to mess up." He closed the gap between them and cut off further discussion. Talk was overrated, especially at a time like this, when he half expected his jeans to start coming apart at the seams.

Garrett bucked up toward him, and Aubrey worked his hands down his back to cup his ass. Those hard globes felt great in his hands, and he kneaded the flesh, wishing there was a way he could get right through the fabric to Garrett's skin beneath.

"Guess I need to do this the old-fashioned way."

"What the hell are you mumbling about?" Garrett asked.

Aubrey grabbed his belt and yanked it open, along with his jeans, and pushed them down before once again taking hold of Garrett's ass, this time stroking hot, bare, smooth flesh. "How good you feel," he rasped and quivered as Garrett reached between them. Garrett pulled and tugged at Aubrey's belt and jeans until he'd relieved some of the intense pressure. Aubrey's cock sprang forward as he lifted his hips. Garrett took advantage of the access and wrapped his fingers around Aubrey's shaft.

"Oh God," Aubrey moaned softly.

"I can agree with that." Garrett shivered when Aubrey teased down his cleft, just glancing around his opening.

"I like the 'Oh God' moments." Aubrey flexed his hips, and Garrett gripped him tighter. He wished he could see what Garrett was doing. He'd love to see his strong, sure hands wrapped around his cock, but it was too dark, so he had to feel it instead. Maybe that was the point and the beauty of being out here. They had to feel, and if that was the case, then Aubrey would make this the best-feeling night either of them had ever had.

Aubrey backed away and rolled Garrett onto his belly, tugging his hips upward. A pale white ass glistened in the darkness like a beacon of loveliness. He parted Garrett's cheeks and buried his face in what he found, licking and sucking, tasting Garrett's heavy musk until the truck shook on its suspension.

"I'm trying not to make noise," Garrett groaned.

"There's nothing around for miles in every direction. You can make as much noise as you want."

He was tired of being quiet and careful about every sound they made. The one time they had gone to Garrett's tiny trailer, they both realized they could hear sounds coming from the main ranch house, so they had to be silent even as Aubrey wanted to shout at the top of his lungs as he came with Garrett deep inside him. Even at the creek they'd had to be careful. After all, if he could hear his mother, then she might be able to hear them. Out here there was only the wind and some cattle that could care less if they shouted their pleasure at the stars.

"No," Garrett said, quaking like the first leaves of spring in the wind. "There's a new house just over the next rise." He tilted his head to the side, and Aubrey growled. That meant they had to be somewhat quiet, or they might arouse suspicions.

"Then your job is to hold in the shout while I make you want to scream your head off."

"Fucker!"

"Exactly what I had planned," Aubrey agreed and went back to eating Garrett out, stroking his ass and back, pushing his legs farther apart.

"Jesus!" Garrett pushed back on his knees, driving harder against Aubrey's tongue. He pulled away and began working out of his pants.

"You got stuff?"

Garrett pressed what he needed into his hand. "When I got the blanket."

"Damn, you're a real Boy Scout." Aubrey tore open the packet and got ready. "I'm not going to last very long."

"Like I am either after how you got me going." Garrett pressed his ass up. Aubrey's hands shook as he tried like hell to finish. He got lube all over the place, but he didn't care. All he wanted was Garrett around him. Finally he was ready, and he got into position and sank into molten heat.

Garrett backed back into him, taking him all at once, stealing Aubrey's breath. "God," Aubrey gasped "Yeah." Garrett held still and then rocked back and forth, moving along Aubrey's cock. Talk about topping from the bottom. Aubrey leaned forward, pressing Garrett into the blankets, and took control, driving into Garrett with all he had. Garrett's muffled cry reached his ears, and Aubrey realized he was screaming into the blankets. He hoped he hadn't hurt him. When Aubrey tried to pull out, Garrett slammed back against him and gave him the answer he needed. From then on, Aubrey let instinct and need take over. He wrapped Garrett in his arms, leaned over his back, and pumped his hips.

"Love feeling you around and in me," Garrett hissed.

"Yeah," Aubrey whispered, sucking on Garrett's ear, listening as he did his best not to make too much noise. It wasn't long before they both gave up on that front. Being with Garrett was too good to keep quiet about. Soon they were keening and moaning like wild animals. At least that's what Aubrey hoped anyone listening would think it was. "That's it, come for me. I can feel you right on the edge."

"How…?"

"You're shaking trying to keep control. Let go," he coaxed, and Garrett's control snapped. Aubrey knew the second it happened. Garrett's quivering intensified, and then he held still, his muscles spasming around Aubrey's cock, clamping down on him tightly. Aubrey closed his eyes, thrust one last time, and followed Garrett into the throes of sweet oblivion.

He didn't want to move an inch; Garrett felt too good. But they slowly sank down onto the blankets, and Aubrey withdrew, taking care of business by tying off the condom and setting it aside, making sure it stayed inside the truck. Then he settled next to Garrett, holding him and letting the night air flow over them.

"You know we're going to have to explain why our clothes are sweated through."

"It was worth it." Aubrey pulled off his shirt and set it aside. It was wringing wet. Too late now, but he knew he should have taken it off. Things had happened too quickly. He helped Garrett with his and hung them on the side of the truck, then lay down next to him once again. He took Garrett's hand and stared up at the stars. "I used to dream of being an astronaut."

"You did?" Garrett asked.

"Yeah. I figured that was as far away from this town as I could possibly get." He turned as he chuckled. "To think I came right back."

"I never really left. I tried school, but it didn't work out. Didn't last a semester." Garrett rolled onto his side. "With the way my folks are, I thought in high school that I'd be on the first bus out of town as soon as I could. But I got a good job that I really love."

"Yeah, I know. There's something about the land that gets in your soul. I didn't understand until I figured out that the ranch was in trouble and that it could be gone forever. Then I realized what this place meant to me." Who would have thought someone he'd known most of his life would be the one to help make everything worthwhile.

"So I take it you're going to keep the ranch? With your experiences out East and such, I thought you might turn it around and keep it going for your folks, then sell it as a healthy business."

"No. It's mine, and it will stay that way. Carolann isn't interested in it." He'd already put so much of his blood, sweat, and pride into the place that he couldn't give it up. "It's mine now. Mom and Dad have already said so." Well, they hadn't transferred it to him legally, but his dad had said their will reflected who had come to their aid. Not that he begrudged Carolann, but when the troubles really started, she'd been supportive but from afar, and she seemed very content for it to remain that way.

"You sound so sure of what you want."

"Aren't you?" Aubrey asked, closing his eyes and letting the air do its drying thing.

"I guess. I always wondered if there wasn't more. I've lived in this town all my life. Yeah, I'm not doing what my dad wanted, because I just couldn't, and I like working with cattle, but I hope to have my own spread someday. Maybe up in Wyoming or something. Hell, I don't know. But this part of Texas is starting to scare me a little." Garrett rolled on his side and lightly stroked his chest. "It's 2015, but these people are still stuck in the sixties. The rest of the country has moved on, but we're still stuck in this time warp where nothing meaningful ever seems to change."

"And Wyoming is any better?"

"I suppose not," Garrett sighed. "But it would be different."

"I don't know about different, but it would be nice if folks could just let folks be. Everybody is so worried about what everybody else is doing and looking over their shoulder. Most folks are nice enough, but if they knew… about us… would they talk about us behind our backs, or would those same nice folks be the first ones to try to run us out of town?"

Garrett stayed quiet for a while. "Don't know."

"When I was in school in Austin, things were different, easier. People there are more accepting. It's the funky part of the state. I liked it there and might have stayed. School itself was hard, but life in general was easier. After I left school, I ended up in Baltimore, but that just made things worse." There was no use regretting what was. He'd come home and had made his bed. The life he might have had was gone now. "I used to go out with friends, and no one cared. We were a few blocks from the state capitol building, where politicians were railing against people like us, and there we were, dancing and having a good time, flipping the idiots the bird."

"Reality is sometimes so different from what we hope. We can get married here now, but that still doesn't change anything. Just paints a public target on our backs… at least out here." Garrett seemed to feel the same way he did. "I heard that even in Dallas, folks are starting to get riled up about places that have been there for years."

Nothing surprised Aubrey anymore. He figured he'd try to keep his head low, do what he needed to, and then come back here to figure out the rest of his life. He turned to face Garrett and kissed him slowly, deeply, trying to put his worries out of his mind. For right this moment, he had Garrett, they were alone, and nothing could burst the happy bubble they were in. He knew it was too bad things couldn't stay like that all the time, but reality was sometimes an awful bitch.

Chapter Eight

"ARE you going to Dallas this weekend?" his mother asked as she carried a basket of dirty laundry down the hallway.

"Yes. But I think this will be the last time for a while."

His mom shook her head. "I'd think if you spent so much time with these friends that you'd be a little less chipper about not seeing them as much any longer."

He should have known his mother would notice just about everything. "Things have changed. I don't think I need to spend as much time down there." He tried to keep the relief out of his voice. She needed to think everything was normal, even though he was so filled with relief he could barely stand it. The pressing bills were paid, he had some extra money in the bank, and Saturday was the last time he'd need to dance in front of strangers.

"So does this mean that you've found a reason to stay here instead of going to Dallas?" A smile curved her pink-lipsticked mouth. "Is it too much to hope that you've met a girl here in town and that you're going to settle down here?"

"Is that what this is all about? You think I'm not settled here and that if I get married, I'll be more likely to stay?"

She set down the basket. "I just want you to be happy."

Aubrey noticed the way she found the wallpaper behind him interesting. "Mom."

"Well, you left and only came back when we were in trouble." She sniffled. "Oh, I told myself I wasn't going to do this. Your father and I can't keep up the ranch on our own. The house…. It's more than I can take care of any longer."

"What do you mean?"

"There's dust under the beds, and if you look under the living room furniture…. I used to be able to really clean the house and cook, do the laundry. When was the last time you weren't the first one up?"

"So you sleep later—"

"I'm getting old." She made it sound like it was the end of everything.

"Yes, you are. And that means you should be cleaning less and that you and Dad should go out to eat a little more. Maybe take a trip, just the two of you."

"I don't want to go anywhere. This is home. But I…. You need to be taken care of so if something happens to your father and me…. So you won't be alone. Life is long if you don't have someone who cares."

"Mom. I'm not going to be alone, and you don't need to push people at me. I have friends, and I'll find someone. Just worry less about me and enjoy your life. That's what's important to me and why I came back to help you." The thought of his mom and dad being thrown out of their home still worried him.

"I'll try."

"Okay. And if you're worried about the housecleaning, maybe in a few months we can get someone in to help you." Aubrey knew how that would go over, and he wasn't disappointed.

"I'm not having some stranger in my house." She stared daggers at him. "I'd have to go through and make sure everything was spotless before she came."

"Okay, Mom." He turned away with a smile.

"And don't think I don't know what you're doing." She picked up the clothes basket and marched away. Aubrey watched her go, shaking his head. Sometimes his mother was as big a mystery to him as anything in life.

"Where's Dad?" Aubrey called as he walked through the living room.

"He said he was going to go out and check on the herd," his mother answered, and then the washing machine switched on.

Aubrey stepped outside and walked to the equipment shed. Inside he found a large empty space where the tractor had been. He listened for the engine, in case his dad wasn't too far away, but he heard nothing. Knowing his dad had done this work all his life, Aubrey went into the barn to get his chores done.

"Aubrey," his mother called, panic clear. "It's your father."

He raced over to her, and she handed him the phone. "Dad!" Aubrey said loudly, but all he heard was air rushing through the line.

"I heard him groan and then nothing." His mom was shaking, so Aubrey got her settled in a chair on the porch. He handed her the phone.

"Don't hang it up." Aubrey pulled his own out of his pocket and called Garrett. "Something's wrong. Dad is out somewhere."

"What happened?"

"I don't know. He called but doesn't seem able to talk."

"I'm on my way. Call the police." Garrett hung up, and Aubrey called 911. He explained what he knew and stayed on the line until sirens sounded in the distance. Garrett pulled in the drive a few minutes before the police.

"Did Dad say where he was going exactly?" Aubrey asked his mother, who shook her head. "Then we have to go look for him."

"We will. I have other units on the way," the police officer said. He wasn't anyone Aubrey was familiar with. The officer made radio calls. He also took the phone, listened, and kept the line open, though Aubrey suspected that out here it would be nearly impossible to follow the signal. More police cars pulled into the drive, and they conferenced quickly before the units pulled away again, heading out.

"I'm going to look too," Garrett said.

Aubrey looked at his mother. He wanted to try to find his father as well, but he was also concerned about leaving his mother alone.

"I'll call my mom and have her come over," Garrett offered. Aubrey's mother nodded, and he hurried with Garrett toward his truck.

"Head south," Aubrey told Garrett. "That's where the herd was yesterday, and I doubt they've moved very much, so it's the most likely direction."

Garrett nodded, already on the phone. "Mom, I need you to come and sit with Mrs. Klein. We think something has happened to Mr. Klein, and we don't want her to be alone." Garrett listened for a few seconds and then hung up. "She's on her way."

They reached the end of the driveway, and Garrett gunned the engine. Aubrey sat, hands fidgeting in his lap as he tried to think of where his father could be. "Turn left up ahead. There's an access road, and he may have gone down there." As they approached, a police vehicle was coming out. They slowed, and the officer shook his head. "Then continue on." Garrett nodded and floored it.

At the next turnoff, they made a left down the track. The police vehicle continued on down the road. "Over there," Garrett said, speeding up. It took a second before Aubrey understood what they were seeing. A tractor wheel, high in the air.

"Shit," Aubrey swore, his heart racing, sweat breaking out on his brow. He got on the phone and called the police to let them know where they were. Sirens followed them, and by the time Aubrey and Garrett stopped and got out, other cars were right behind them.

The tractor seemed to have gone off the track and then rolled sideways down an incline. It wasn't that steep and only about thirty feet, but it was enough to roll the tractor.

Aubrey jumped out and slid down the hill, racing to the tractor. The cab was empty. He began looking all around. "Dad!" No answer. His first thought was that he was buried, but there was no sign of him. "Dad, can you hear me?"

There was no answer, and Aubrey retraced the path of the tractor. Others joined him.

"Dad!" Aubrey felt panic begin to rise as a shoe sticking out from the underbrush caught his eye. "Over here. Get the ambulance."

"They're on their way," an officer told him as more sirens got closer and closer.

"Dad," Aubrey said as he fell to his knees next to his dad. People rushed past him and gently moved Aubrey out of the way.

"Let us help him," a gentle voice said. Aubrey barely heard it, all his attention on his father as he lay in the brush. "He's alive," one of them said. Aubrey couldn't see much blood, and he hoped that was a good sign.

Garrett joined him, already on the phone. "We found him and he's alive. We're not sure what's wrong. The ambulance is here, and we'll stop by to pick you up on our way back." Garrett hung up. "My mom is at the house with your mom."

"Aubrey," one of the EMTs said. "He's asking for you."

He hurried over and fell to his knees next to his dad, who had already been attached to a back board and had a neck brace on. "Tell your mother not to worry. I'm going to be okay." He was blinking like crazy.

"We think he might have a head injury. The rest is a precaution."

"Is he cut?"

"Just some scrapes, as far as we can tell. Your dad was very lucky. He was thrown out. We're going to transport him to Greenville Memorial."

"Okay," Aubrey said, tears welling in his eyes. "You're going to be okay, Dad."

"I know, son."

Aubrey touched his father's hand and then let go so they could carry him out and away. Once his father was gone, Aubrey turned to what was left of the tractor. It had rolled once and lay on its side. Even he could see that the front bucket attachment was bent and that there was little left of the cab.

"It is insured," Garrett said.

"Yeah." But in order to keep costs down, the deductible was set pretty high, so he would have to come up with a couple thousand dollars. That was if it could be repaired. If not, he'd get what it was worth, and then he'd have to buy another tractor. Either way…. Aubrey pushed that out of his mind. "Let's go get Mom so we can meet them there."

Garrett nodded.

"Would you like us to call Grayson's to have the tractor pulled out and towed back to your place?" the police officer who'd taken charge back at the ranch asked.

"That would be great."

"Be sure to call the insurance company. Most of them work with Grayson's, so that shouldn't be an issue."

"Thanks." Aubrey could hardly put two thoughts together. He was numb and still worried about his father.

"Go on. I have your number, and I'll take care of things here."

Aubrey nodded and walked in a daze toward Garrett's truck. He got in and stared out the window until Garrett got in. Garrett drove them back to the ranch. As soon as they arrived, their mothers joined them. Aubrey got in the cramped backseat of the super cab with his mom and explained what he'd been told as they rode.

Town had never seemed so far away, and even though Garrett was driving as fast as he could, it seemed like they were barely moving at all. Finally, they pulled into the hospital parking lot.

"Go on in. I'll park and find you," Garrett told them all. Aubrey helped his mother inside and got her seated before approaching the desk and explaining why they were there.

"We'll be with you very soon," the receptionist told him and made a call back. "He's with the doctor now."

IT took hours, but in the end, the doctor came out with the news that his dad was going to be okay. Aubrey's back-aching tension broke when he got the news. They wanted to keep his father for a few days to make sure he was truly all right, and that there wasn't any swelling on his brain from the concussion. Aubrey's mom was going to stay with him, so once Aubrey said good-bye, he rode back to the ranch with Garrett.

Aubrey wandered the ranch yard, stopping by what was left of the tractor. He could see it was a total loss already. The thing was old to begin with. He and his dad had kept it running and working through sheer force of will and careful maintenance for almost two years.

"Are you going to be okay?" Garrett asked. Aubrey nodded and walked toward the barn. "I'll help you."

"Don't you have your own work to do?" Aubrey didn't mean it as snappy as the words came out, but he saw Garrett blanch.

"I called while I was at the hospital. Bridger said to help here with anything you need. If you don't want me to stay, just say so, and I'll take off."

Aubrey didn't move for a long time. "I better get these chores done." It was all he could think about. And he was grateful, more grateful than he could ever form into words, when Garrett followed him into the barn.

He fed and watered all the horses while Garrett spot-cleaned stalls and brought in more bedding. The list of things he'd needed to do had been huge, but that had all changed in a few hours.

"You need to remember to call the insurance company," Garrett told him gently as he closed the door on the last stall. "Bridger said he has a tractor you can borrow for a week or so, until you can get another."

Aubrey wanted to cry, but he'd be damned if that was going to happen. "Please tell him that I'd appreciate that very much." At least he was going to be able to see to it that the herd was taken care of. He was damn near overwhelmed.

"Come on." Garrett took him by the shoulders, pointing him toward the door. "You need to go inside, make the calls that are important, and then give yourself a few minutes to breathe."

Aubrey nodded and followed Garrett's instructions. Inside, he made his calls. The insurance agent got him in touch with the adjuster, and he said he'd send someone out. But he wasn't too hopeful. He said with the high deductible and the damage Aubrey described that the tractor was most likely a total loss. His hope that somehow it could be repaired had been fleeting at best, and now his worst fears were nearing reality. A new tractor would cost more money than they had, even after the insurance payout. Still, he consoled himself that his father was going to be okay. That was what mattered.

He wandered out of the office and found Garrett on the sofa watching television with the volume turned low. "I wasn't sure about leaving you alone. You seemed… out of it."

"Thanks." He came around and sat next to him. "I don't know what I'm going to do."

"Everything will be fine."

Aubrey didn't see how it could be.

"Mom called a little while ago," Garrett said. "Dad came to the hospital, and he's going to bring our moms home. They're both apparently very tired, and now that they know your dad will be okay, they want your mom to get some rest."

At least he didn't have to drive back in to pick them up. He would have, but it was nice not to have to. "I'll be sure to thank your dad."

"Do you want me to stay?"

He really did. "I don't want to keep you from what you need to do. There's nothing any of us can do now but wait for stuff to happen." That was always the worst situation to be in. Nothing was in his control, and all he could do was wait to see what the hell would happen next. "If you need to leave, I'll understand."

Garrett shifted closer. "What I want to do is stay and make sure you're going to be okay."

"I will." Still, he leaned closer to Garrett and closed his eyes, trying to push away the worry. "Now that Dad's going to be okay, I'm wondering how I'm going to afford a new piece of equipment." He hated to give voice to it, because his dad was what was important, he knew that, but the financial implication of this accident couldn't be ignored.

"I know things have been tough for you, but weren't you just saying that the ranch is getting back on its feet?"

"Yeah. But with this I'm right back where I was." He closed his eyes. This was supposed to have been his last weekend at the club. That part of his life was supposed to be over, and once again he'd be able to look himself in the eye without seeing someone he didn't like. He could reclaim his pride and go back to just being a rancher and a cowboy. Now there was a tractor that was going to cost thousands, maybe tens of thousands, and that was going to have to be paid for… somehow. The ranch budgets had been stretched, but they'd almost been in a place where they could live and even pull themselves into a good place.

"Things will work out. You worked your way out of it before. You'll do it again."

Aubrey nodded. That was, of course, the only answer. He had to continue dancing if they were to have any hope of a future. The balls he'd spent months juggling, and thought he could put to rest, had just been thrown back into the air—only now there were more of them. To make matters worse, Aubrey was tired.

Garrett lightly touched his chin, and Aubrey turned in that direction. Garrett leaned closer, kissing him gently at first, but deepening it quickly. Aubrey tugged at Garrett's shirt, pulling him on top as he fell back onto the sofa cushions. "We can't do this," Garrett whispered.

"I know." Aubrey sighed softly and held Garrett close, burying his face in Garrett's shoulder. He needed some time to get his thoughts together so he could figure out what the hell he was going to do.

"Things will work out. You work too hard for them not to."

"I sure as hell hope so." He leaned back, kissing Garrett as tires on gravel sounded outside. Aubrey didn't want to pull away, but he had no choice, and by the time his mother came in, Aubrey sat trying to pay attention to what was on television.

"How's Dad?" he asked.

"I think he's going to be fine," she answered, looking tired and drawn, dark circles under her eyes and worry crinkling her lips. "Thank you for taking us, Garrett."

"Aren't Mom and Dad coming in?" Garrett asked, standing to look out the window.

"Your dad said he needed to be at the church in half an hour for a meeting. So he was going to take your mother home and go on."

"A meeting…." Garrett shook his head, and Aubrey wondered what that was about. "I should get going, but if you need anything, either of you, please call me."

His mom went to Garrett, and he bent down so she could hug him. "Thank you for everything. You're a good boy." She backed away and patted Garrett's cheek. "I was always happy that you and Aubrey were friends."

"Even when he and I nearly caused a stampede?" Garrett asked.

"Don't be smart," she said with a genuine smile. "Life with you two was never dull, I'll give you that. But you both grew up to be fine men." She opened her purse and pulled out a tissue, dabbing the corners of her eyes. "I need to lie down for a while."

"I'll be here, Mom," Aubrey said. His mother nodded and walked toward the hallway. Aubrey accompanied Garrett to the door.

"I know my mom said just about everything, but thank you."

"You know I'll be here for you." Garrett stepped outside, and Aubrey was about to close the door when Garrett stopped him. "I was wondering if you were going in to Dallas on Saturday? I thought if it was okay, I'd go with you. I think it could be fun to meet your friends."

Aubrey didn't know exactly what to say. "I don't know," he lied, feeling like a huge pile of shit for doing it. Garrett nodded, and Aubrey closed the door. The balls he'd been juggling just multiplied one more time.

Chapter Nine

"ARE you comfortable?" Aubrey asked his dad early on Saturday morning.

"I'm not an invalid," his dad snapped. He'd been home from the hospital for a day, and he'd managed to yell at Mom, him, and even Garrett when he came over the day before to see how he was doing. "Did that shyster from the insurance company call you back?"

"Dad. Shysters are lawyers."

"Doesn't matter. He's trying to cheat us. That tractor was worth a lot more than three thousand dollars."

Aubrey sighed.

"You disagreeing with me, boy?" He leaned forward in his chair, eyes as hard as nails.

"The deductible was two thousand dollars, so they valued the tractor at five thousand." Which was probably being damned generous. But his father didn't want to hear that. "You need to let me handle this." The paperwork had already arrived, so he hoped his father would calm down and see reason. "I'm looking at replacements."

His father humphed, which was exactly how Aubrey felt. There was nothing available that wasn't thousands of dollars more than they had.

"Barney, there's no need to be nasty. I know you aren't feeling well, but the doctors said you need to take it easy."

"Helen…."

She stormed over. "I've had it with this attitude of yours. Yeah, you cracked up the tractor. That's no reason to take things out on us. So you feel bad. That doesn't mean you get to make the rest of us miserable." She crossed her arms, and his dad stared back at her for about two seconds before sighing and leaning back in his chair. "I'll get you some tea, and you can have a rest." She left the room, lightly patting Aubrey on the shoulder.

"I hope you have a rabbit to pull out of the hat on this one, because the money for a tractor isn't going to just appear," his dad mumbled. "I should have stayed here in this damn chair."

"Dad, it was an accident."

"So we've gone from anger to self-pity, have we?" his mother said as she handed him a mug. "It doesn't suit you, so adjust the attitude, feel better, and we'll go on the way we always have. There's nothing we can't do if we work together." She patted his dad's shoulder. "Are you still going to Dallas?"

"Unless you need me here," Aubrey said. He really did need to go. Tonight could be worth a thousand dollars, and they needed the money, but the trips to Dallas had always been "to see friends." So while they were really important, he couldn't let on that they were or it would raise suspicions.

"Your dad and I aren't going anywhere, and he is probably going to spend most of the evening sleeping in his chair, so you might as well go and have some fun." She turned to leave. "Is Garrett going with you?"

He still hadn't figured out the excuse he was going to use to get Garrett to stay here. He'd been racking his brain, but he couldn't come up with anything that wouldn't hurt his feelings.

Chapter Ten

WHAT the hell was he going to do? Aubrey had
been stupid enough to tell Garrett that he could come
to Dallas with him. He took a deep breath and began
pacing his room. Maybe it was time for him to come
clean and just tell Garrett what he'd been doing and
why. The thought scared the living hell out of him.
Garrett had said he was the one person he could rely on,
and he knew what Garrett thought of guys who worked
at the club. He'd tried to pick him up that first night.
Aubrey knew now: Garrett was not going to take his
deception well.

"You're going to wear a hole in the carpet," his
mother scolded as she walked by without stopping.
Aubrey stopped pacing and sat on the edge of the bed.
There was no good solution to his problem. Maybe he

should just call the club and say he wasn't coming in. Then he could call Garrett and tell him that his plans had changed and he wasn't going into Dallas after all. Aubrey breathed deeply as some of the tension ebbed away. That had to be the answer he was looking for.

He stood and left his room, wandering out to check on his dad, who was asleep in his chair. He sputtered awake and sat up, coughing.

"Do you need something to drink?" Aubrey asked him.

He nodded, and Aubrey jogged into the kitchen. He filled a glass with water, brought it to his dad, and then returned to the kitchen to go through the mail. There was a letter from the insurance company explaining their offer and what he needed to do. Aubrey had managed to get them to come up a couple hundred dollars, but that was all.

"Clive Coleson called," his mother said as she came into the kitchen. "He says he has a used tractor in good shape that just came in." His mother sat down at the table. "He said it's in excellent condition, and that he got a good price on it. He's willing to give us first chance, and he said because he got a deal, he could do well by us."

"Did he say how much it was?"

"He said he could sell it for fifteen, but for us, he'd go twelve." She grinned.

"Why would he do that?" Aubrey understood helping a neighbor, but that seemed a little too good to be true. His mother simply smiled and left the room. "Okay. Tell him I'll be in to see him on Monday."

"Okay," she agreed, and Aubrey went through the rest of the mail, thankful there were no unexpected bills in the pile. He stacked the envelopes and sat down, wondering what he was going to do. Nine grand. He had to either borrow nine grand or figure something out. The small nest egg he'd managed to pull together wouldn't come close to covering the cost of the new tractor. He knew the books for the ranch by heart. There was no room in the budget for another payment. He had to go into Dallas. That was the only way he could make this work.

The back screen door squeaked open and snapped shut. "Morning, Garrett, are you staying for lunch?"

"I wish I could." Garrett strode in. "I stopped in to say I can't go to Dallas with you. Mr. Bridger's daughter, Brianne—you probably know her, right? Well, she fell off her horse, and he stepped on her leg. Bridger's on his way to the hospital with her. Looks real bad, and she may need surgery."

"Poor little thing," his mother said and began fussing in the kitchen. "You come back this afternoon, and I'll have something for you to take over to the family. They'll be too busy and all." She didn't finish her thought, but Aubrey understood.

"Do they think she'll be okay?" Aubrey covered the relief he felt.

"They do. But I saw her fall off and heard the crack." Garrett shivered. "Anyway, I need to cover at the ranch since he's going to be shorthanded today. I was looking forward to meeting your friends, but there will be another time, I'm sure."

"Of course," Aubrey said, knowing he was only putting off the problem until later. "Do you want me to stay?"

"Course not. Go on in like you planned." Garrett paused, and Aubrey knew there was more he wanted to say, but couldn't. "No need to disappoint your friends."

Shit, that made him feel worse for what he was going to do. "I can help."

"No. It's okay." Garrett checked his watch. "I need to get back." He headed through the house, and Aubrey followed him outside.

"Text me and let me know how she's doing," Aubrey said as they strode to Garrett's truck.

"I surely will." Garrett pulled open his door, and Aubrey stepped out of the way and waited. "I'm sorry I can't go—"

"Hey, it's all right." Shit, Aubrey felt even worse. Garrett was upset because he couldn't go, and all Aubrey could think about was how relieved he was. This was truly fucked-up, and it was all his own stupid fault. He'd been so close to bringing all this to an end he could taste it, but now…. "You'll come with me another time. I'll be back tomorrow morning, and maybe we can go to lunch and for a ride in the afternoon."

"I'd like that," Garrett told him softly, and Aubrey wished he could try to comfort him. "I really wanted to meet your friends. You spend enough time with them…." Garrett plopped his hat on his head. "It sort of feels like you have another life that I'm not part of." Garrett got in the truck, pulling the door closed with a deep thud. Aubrey stood back, watching Garrett pull away. Fucking hell, he did have a separate part of himself—a whole part of his life that none of them knew about… and hopefully never would.

THE trip to Dallas felt somber, as if he were going to a funeral. Aubrey felt none of the illusion of freedom he'd had all those months ago when he'd first started. This job had been a chance to get out of debt and remove the dagger of financial ruin and the loss of his family legacy. At least that was how it had started out. Now when Aubrey pulled up to the club, he saw it for what it was: just a place where guys took their clothes off for money. The relatively nondescript building in the gay section of town had at first seemed exotic and different from anything else in his life.

He parked his truck and put on his mask. Then he got out and went inside, noticing the stains and discolored paint.

"I was beginning to think you weren't coming," Barry said in his usual light tone, but there was something behind his eyes that Aubrey hadn't noticed before: exhaustion. Maybe it had always been there, but he just hadn't seen it.

"I got started a little later than usual." He kept to himself and went right in to get changed. "Are we keeping the same order as last week?" Aubrey asked when Barry followed him, stripping down to change.

"Yes," he answered and turned. "What happened, kid? You look like hammered shit."

"My dad rolled the tractor and ended up with a concussion." He rarely talked about anything personal in anything other than generic terms. "It's been a hard week, but I'll be fine." Aubrey smiled, but it wasn't genuine. He doubted with all the activity around him in the relatively cramped space that anyone either noticed or cared.

Aubrey did his numbers, hearing the screams and calls of the men in the audience, but now it felt like there was an invisible wall between them and him. He used to get energy from the crowd, and they would push him on. Now that wall prevented almost all of it. He knew exactly what that wall was, and it had a name:

Garrett. He didn't want to be here. At one time he thought he might have actually enjoyed the attention, liked something beyond the money. But now that was all it was. Oh, he kept his head about him and did what was expected, slinking through the crowd, grinding his hips, letting guys place bills a little too close for comfort. It was all part of the game. Once or twice he even pushed the envelope, tugging at his thong just enough to give the illusion of a sneak peek. Of course, they saw nothing more than normal, but the tips and bills sure reflected what he'd done.

"Barry was right. Hammered shit," Simon said as he sat down between shows once they'd changed and were waiting to do it all over again.

"What?" Aubrey asked, hearing what was going on around him for the first time.

"If this isn't fun any longer, and you aren't happy, then you definitely need to move on." Simon bumped his shoulder while the other guys talked and gossiped. "You looked as good out there as you always did, but back here, you talk even less than usual."

"Sorry. I didn't mean to be antisocial."

"I heard what you said to Barry. If this whole family thing you have going is getting to be too much and you have to choose, for God's sake don't choose this."

"You seem to be happy enough."

Simon chuckled. "Yeah, but I'm a complete slut." He bumped Aubrey's shoulder once again. "This isn't for you. I know you're here for the money to help your family, but it seems to be tearing you apart." Aubrey didn't say anything. "Do what you want. I only came over because I thought you could use a friend." Simon pushed his chair back and stood up. He was about to step away when Aubrey reached out and grabbed his wrist.

"Thanks," he said, forcing another smile. Simon nodded, and Aubrey let his hand fall back to his side. Then he did his best to push everything from his mind so he could get ready to do it all over again.

By the time the second show was over, Aubrey had made more money than usual. He drove back to his hotel and fell into bed, alone. That was the kicker. He was so damned tired of being alone. As tired as he was, he stared up at the ceiling. All he kept thinking about was Garrett. He wished he could have brought him to Dallas and that they could spend the night in this room, together. The juggling act he'd been doing was wearing him out completely. He'd already done what he'd set out to do, and he had some more money with him that he could put toward the new equipment.

This all had to end. He had to get his life back under one roof again. He'd been split in two directions—if he included Garrett, three—for quite a while, and he was starting to splinter. His essence, his soul, was starting to suffer. Fuck, he didn't even know who the hell he was. Aubrey had always thought of himself as a good person, and yet he'd lied to everyone in his life. He'd even been lying to himself for so long he was starting to believe his own rationalizations.

Eventually he closed his eyes, starting to get sleepy. He knew what he'd do. As soon as he got home, he was going to sit down, put pencil to paper, and figure out a way out of this mess that would leave his family whole, this cracked life of his behind, and would allow him to have Garrett in his life. That was the trifecta as far as he was concerned. He couldn't juggle forever, so he had to bring this act to an end.

Chapter Eleven

"THERE'S your new tractor," Clive said as he jumped down from it after bringing it out to the ranch.

"Do you always deliver?" Aubrey's father said as they shook hands.

"Nope. But Helen promised me some of her apple pie when I was out here next, and this seemed like the fastest way to get here." Clive shook Aubrey's hand as well as his mother's. She beamed from ear to ear and then slapped his shoulder before inviting him inside.

"I know you're worried," his dad said once they were out of earshot. "We need this to get the work done."

Aubrey knew that. "I don't disagree. I was only hoping the old one would last another year." He figured there was no use saying anything more. It would only upset his dad, and that wasn't what he wanted.

"I heard you got a new toy," Garrett called and then slammed his truck door. Aubrey turned and smiled, forgetting himself for a second.

"I'm going inside for pie. Both of you hurry along before Clive eats it all." His dad headed inside.

Aubrey turned to Garrett. "I missed you Sunday." He kept his voice low.

"I had to stay and work. Mr. Bridger is sick with worry. Brianne isn't doing well. They're going to do another operation to try to improve the circulation in her leg. They had to rebuild the bones, but now they're afraid there isn't enough blood getting to the leg for it to heal. So after all that, she could lose the leg."

"Damn," Aubrey swore softly.

"He's been spending all his time at the hospital, so I've been putting in extra hours to cover."

"I could have helped."

"You've got all you can handle here." Garrett looked toward the house. "Your mom and dad are busy at the moment. Can you take a ride?"

"Sure. You start saddling the horses, and I'll let them know I'm going to be out for a while so they don't worry." *Or wonder what's going on.* He went inside and found all three of them eating at the kitchen table.

"Garrett and I are going to go for a ride. I thought I'd check the fences to the north while I was out." He lightly kissed his mother on the cheek.

"Don't forget you promised to take me in to church tonight."

"I don't remember that," Aubrey said as he searched his memory. Then he remembered—it was another of those Lonely Hearts things. He'd heard something about it at the social. His mother must have volunteered to help. "Besides, I have work I have to do tonight."

"Leave the boy alone, Helen. I'll take you in as long as I get fed." His dad leaned back in his chair, patting his belly. It was certainly nice to see some of his old spark had come back.

"The whole idea is for Aubrey to meet someone nice." She glared at her husband, but he didn't back down.

"He can meet someone when he's ready. You're just being a busybody, and it's not attractive." His dad winked at him, and they shared a moment. "Go on and have a good time."

"Thanks," Aubrey said and then left as quickly as he could. Returning to the barn, he found the horses saddled and Garrett ready and waiting for him. "We'd better get out of here. My mother is matchmaking again, and I bet your mother isn't far behind."

"The potluck dinner?" Garrett asked.

Aubrey nodded. "If we're not around, we can't go." He grinned and led his horse out into the yard, mounted, and took off across the field. Garrett came up beside him and then raced ahead. "So that's how it is," he called and spurred his horse faster. He whooped at the top of his lungs.

"What was that for?" Garrett asked when they pulled to a stop.

"It felt good. Freeing." He wished he had a better explanation, but that was all he could come up with. The sun, the wind, flying over the ground on the back of such power—all of it reached down deep inside him, and the cry was the result.

"So you're feeling better?"

"I think so, yeah." Aubrey smiled, and it felt reasonably genuine. "Since Dad got hurt, it's been like the walls are closing in around me." He climbed down and led his horse into the trees.

"You're taking on way too much."

Aubrey stopped. "How so?" He turned to where Garrett was leading Klondike.

"I know the ranch is important to you, but you aren't responsible for the mess. You didn't create it, so you don't need to kill yourself to fix it."

"It's my ranch, or it will be. If I want there to be anything at all, I have to see to it myself." He was getting angry, and he didn't want to be. "This land is my heritage. It's the connection I have with my parents and grandparents. They started it, and if I want it to continue, I have to manage and care for it." He turned and led Marigold the last little bit down to the creek. Then he tied her to a tree in the clearing and sat on the old log near the running water, waiting for Garrett.

"You may be right," Garrett said. "I've never had anything like the ranch. I just grew up in a ranch house, remember?"

Aubrey chuckled. "You had the house, but not the rest of it."

"I guess." Garrett sat down next to him. "I'm worried that you're trying to do too much. You're never around, and when you do get some down time, you run off to Dallas." Aubrey glanced over, but Garrett didn't look at him. "Is there something that I'm not doing? Or am I somehow not good enough for you?" Garrett sighed. "Maybe we should have remained friends, and anything more was just a stupid mistake."

Silence settled between them. Aubrey didn't know what the hell to say. "Do you believe that?" he asked.

"I don't know what to think. Between work, our meddling mothers, and the fact that we don't want everyone in town to know our business, we only have so much time together, and you spend a lot of your free time in Dallas with your friends." Garrett shrugged. "I keep thinking that it's your way of keeping things from only going so far. And if that's what you want, then say so, and I'll back away."

Aubrey's chest ached at the thought. That was why he hadn't told him what he was really doing in Dallas. He was sure that if Garrett knew, he'd leave him, and now it looked like Garrett was going to do that anyway. No matter what, he couldn't win. "If I didn't want you around and I didn't care, I'd say so." He was trying to be truthful above all else, but it was getting harder and harder. What he'd always been told was so very true: lies bred lies, and he was up to his ears in them.

"Then what is it you want?" Garrett's eyes were huge, and the urgency in his voice made Aubrey's heart ache even more. "Have you thought about just telling our families the truth?"

Aubrey gasped and then began to cough. Garrett lightly patted his back until he could catch his breath. "You think your mother and the deacon are ever going to accept that you're gay? My mother wants grandchildren so badly she can taste it, and they both have been pushing us at every single woman within forty miles…. My dad would come unglued, and he might even throw me off the ranch." A ranch he'd given his blood, sweat, tears, and pride to try to save.

Garrett slumped forward a little. "So I'm not worth being honest about."

Aubrey put his arm around Garrett's shoulder. "You are." He breathed and knew it was the truth. "But is that what you really want right now?" Aubrey was afraid of the answer. His foot quivered in the dirt, and he forced it still when Garrett looked at it.

"You're so scared of anyone finding out about you that the notion makes you twitch." He shook his head, and they remained quiet for the longest minute Aubrey had ever felt in his life. He got the feeling they were at some sort of crossroads, and the next few minutes would tell him whether Garrett would remain in his life or if they would have to somehow find their way back to only being friends. "It scares me too." Garrett pulled off his hat and set it on the log next to him, then brushed his hand through his hair. "I don't know what to do, but I know I'm tired of being alone all the time."

Aubrey slowly nodded. "I understand that. Over the past few months, I haven't felt alone very often. There have been a lot of times that I wished you were with me, but I haven't felt nearly as alone as I did."

"We only get to see each other a few times a week," Garrett said.

"Maybe. But I know you're there." He wasn't sure how else to explain it. "Just knowing I have you makes me feel less alone." He turned on the log so he could see Garrett better. "You may be a few miles away when I go to bed most nights, but I know where you are, and my last thought at night is of you. Even when I'm gone, I think about you." God, that was so the truth.

"I think about you too," Garrett said. "I really do. But I'm tired of going home every night, wishing things in my life were different instead of figuring out a way to change them." Garrett picked up his hat and used it to fan away some insects that had decided to take an interest.

"I get that." Aubrey sighed, realizing he was going to have to take a step forward. "I have plans in

Dallas for the next three weekends, but after that, I'll try to stay here." He could handle three more weeks, and he'd make enough money to have a small cushion, even after paying off the new tractor. Maybe then he'd try to find something local he could do to raise some extra money.

"You mean it?" Garrett asked, a smile brightening his face.

"Yeah, I do. I think you're right. It's time I spent more time closer to home and the people I care about." He closed his eyes and released a deep, slow breath. Now that he'd made the promise out loud, there was no going back on it.

Garrett leaned closer, and Aubrey slid his hand around Garrett's neck, drawing him in for a kiss that quickly grew heated. He wanted to be able to do this whenever he wanted, like any other couple, but that was a ways off in this part of the country. Still, it would be nice to be able to come home and have Garrett there every night.

"Sometimes I wonder if all we need to do is cowboy up and just be honest, let the chips fall where they may," Garrett said, a shudder running through him. "There will be folks who hate us, but I'm willing to bet that there will be others who wouldn't give a shit."

"That's true. But we both know that the people who will hate us will be vocal and could turn mean." Aubrey held Garrett's neck, leaning their heads together. "What if we tell my mom and dad and they're okay with it?"

"Do you think that's possible?"

"It snowed here once, so anything is possible. But let's say that's what happens. How many friends will they lose? How hard will that make their lives, and what if people decide not to do business with them?"

Garrett nodded and after a few seconds bumped his shoulder. "I think that's part of why I care about you so much. You're always thinking of everyone else instead of yourself."

"Don't believe that," he responded honestly. "I'm not perfect in that area. I have my own secrets, just like I'm sure you have yours." He wanted to ask Garrett about those secrets, but he wasn't willing to share his. Hell, he simply wanted to put his biggest secret behind him, and in the last few minutes he'd made the decision that he would do just that.

"I hope we can share those secrets," Garrett said, and Aubrey nodded. Maybe someday he'd be able to tell Garrett all about the one decision he'd made and regretted. Yet he wasn't sure he wouldn't make the same one all over again given the circumstances.

"Yeah. I want to get to know everything about you." Aubrey smiled wickedly and ran his fingers lightly behind Garrett's ear. Garrett shivered, and Aubrey did it again. "I like finding those kinds of places. The ones that make your breath hitch."

"I like when you do," Garrett whispered and smacked at his own arm.

Aubrey did the same and backed away. "Dang bugs. Don't they know to leave guys alone when they're kissing?"

"I don't think they got that message," Garrett said, plopping his hat on as he stood. "Maybe we should head back."

Aubrey eyed the water and then Garrett, leaning down to stick his hand in the cool freshness. Then he splashed, sending rivulets toward Garrett. The droplets danced in the streams of light, sparkling before crashing into Garrett's shirt. It was beautiful, especially where the light fabric clung to Garrett's skin.

"Hey! Why'd you do that?"

"You were hot and needed to cool off," Aubrey said. "But then, you're always hot."

Garrett yanked off his boots and socks before bounding toward him and stepping into the creek, his jeans wicking up the water. Not that it mattered, because a wall of water came his way, soaking Aubrey in a matter of seconds. He splashed back, and soon water went everywhere. Aubrey's chuckles turned to full-on laughter, and Garrett joined him. It felt dang good to laugh and let go.

"Okay," Aubrey said, standing up, water dripping from his shirtsleeves and running down his chest and back. He pulled off his hat, slapping it on his arm to get some of the water out.

"You started it," Garrett teased and rushed over, grabbing him around the waist. He lost his balance, and they tumbled to the ground, the shallow creek pooling around them as it paused to rise and gurgle before continuing on its way. Even the water seemed happy.

"What are we going to tell my mother when we get back?" Aubrey asked.

Garrett stood and stepped out of the creek, pulling off his shirt and jeans. He laid them in the sun, standing in his underwear, the excitement from their roughhousing evident. Aubrey undressed as well, laying his clothes next to Garrett's.

"At least you got to take off your boots." He emptied them, shaking his head at the water that poured out. Aubrey set them in the sun and joined Garrett in the shade.

"We're quite a pair, sitting here in our skivvies waiting for our clothes to dry so your mother doesn't get mad at us."

Aubrey couldn't help smiling. "I seem to remember something like this once before. Only then it was because we'd come down here in the spring, and Mom had said the water was too cold. We knew better, of course."

"And you fell in."

"I seem to remember having a little help in that department." He grinned back at Garrett.

"Maybe a little."

Aubrey pushed Garrett, and he rocked back on the ground, laughing. "Asshole. You know you pushed me."

Garrett laughed harder. "And you pulled me in."

"You bet I did." Aubrey's stomach was starting to hurt.

"Yeah, and we tried to dry our clothes in the sun, but a spring storm came up, and we ended up walking back to your house."

"And Momma gave us the tongue lashing of our lives, saying we'd be lucky if we didn't catch pneumonia." He laughed harder.

"Yeah, and I was the one to get a cold that lasted for two weeks. Your mom, of course, told my mom what we'd done, and I got no sympathy at all. I was miserable." Garrett sniffled dramatically.

"Served you right. You were the one who started it." Aubrey continued laughing. "But you weren't the only one who paid. My mother was ready to tan my hide. Instead, I got extra chores for a week, and after that the horse stalls became my permanent job."

"I didn't know that."

"Oh yeah. Momma said if I was going to not listen and give her that kind of grief, then I could shovel shit until I died." Aubrey remembered that conversation all taking place while he was soaking wet, standing on the porch because she wouldn't let him in the house. He'd had to change in the barn. "Carolann thought it was hilarious until Momma caught her laughing. She got stall duty too."

"Do you talk to her much?"

"No. She talks to Momma and Daddy, but mostly she stays away as much as she can. Sometimes I think she's afraid Momma will try to put her to work if she comes around." Their laughter died away. "She and Momma had a fight about something a few years ago, and they talk to each other, but Carolann isn't in any hurry to come visiting." Lord knew he wasn't about to get in the middle of it. The whole thing had disaster written all over it. "I think it had something to do with Momma wanting her to come back and get married. Carolann is never coming back. She has her own life away from what she never liked. Carolann is all about fashion and decorating." Aubrey looked around. "There isn't much of that here."

"Do you miss her?"

"Yeah, I do, and I think Mom and Dad do too, but she's happy, and that's what matters. I bet she'd come home if I asked her, but I never have." Aubrey stared up at the sky through the quaking leaves. "It has to be her decision."

Garrett slid his hand into his, and Aubrey tightened his fingers. The simple touch felt so right. He knew under normal circumstances he'd be raring to go, but this wasn't like that, and it shocked him in a way. It was as though his entire body, even his dick, which reacted when Garrett was upwind of him, realized that just being together, quiet and content, was more important than sex.

"How do you think Carolann would react if she knew about us?"

Aubrey rolled his head so he could see Garrett. "She's the one member of the family I don't have to worry about. She'd support me no matter what." He knew that deep down, without a doubt. "Just like I support her." A sense of contentment washed over him. "But she isn't here."

"But unquestioning support is pretty nice."

"Yeah, it is." Aubrey agreed. "And I know there are more people out there. Carrie, for one." He snickered a little.

"What was up with you two at that social, anyway?"

"I never told you?" Aubrey asked, and Garrett shook his head. "We got along just great. That girl called me out within a few minutes."

"You mean she knew, just like that?" Garrett sat up and looked down at himself as though he'd just sprouted a huge sign that said he liked boys. "How?"

"She likes girls."

"Well, I'll be damned. She told you that?" Garrett asked.

"Yeah. The girl's got balls." Aubrey waited a few seconds, and they both began to laugh. "She's also got the same problem we do. Her mother is pushing her, so we danced, and everyone was happy, and all I could think of at the time was how shocked my mother would be if she knew the truth."

"Everyone would be, and I don't think I wanna be the poster child for gay cowboys in Greenville."

Aubrey rolled onto his side. "We'll figure it out. Once some things are settled and a lot less up in the air, we'll determine what we want to do." Aubrey squeezed Garrett's hand. "There has to be a solution, because I really want to live my life in 2015 rather than in 1955."

"So you do want to come out?" Garrett said.

"Maybe, someday. I don't know. But I do know that whatever happens, I want us to figure it out together." The thought of doing it alone was daunting, but if he and Garrett stood together, then maybe the ordeal could be bearable. Hell, it was only a thought.

"Okay." Garrett went back to looking up at the sky. "I think I'd do a lot so I could have you in my bed every night." Those few words warmed Aubrey's heart faster than the sun in July. That idea sounded so wonderful. But he couldn't have it, at least not now.

"We should see if our clothes are dry," Aubrey said, but he didn't move. He was too content.

"Five more minutes," Garrett said, and Aubrey chuckled, hearing their younger selves asking their mothers to let them play for just a little while longer.

"You can have all the time you want. Hopefully my father has taken my mother in to church and the house will be quiet when we return."

"You know they're pushing us because they care," Garrett said.

"It's easy to forget that sometimes. And maybe, just maybe, it wouldn't hurt us if they cared a little bit less."

"Sometimes you can be a smartass."

"Yeah, I can, but I'm your smartass," Aubrey quipped without thinking.

"Yes." Garrett rolled in his direction, sliding his hand up his arm, tugging Aubrey closer. "You most certainly are." He shifted closer, closing his lips over

Aubrey's, the kiss gentle but filled with heat and longing. As romantic as it might have been to make love out in the open, Aubrey knew it wouldn't be a good idea. He gentled the kiss and then pulled away.

They gazed into each other's eyes, both of them a little breathless. Aubrey didn't have to look to see that Garrett was excited—it was as evident in his eyes, just like Aubrey thought Garrett saw it in his. "We need to go back, or I'm not going to be able to stop." He didn't move and half hoped Garrett would push him onto his back and climb on top of him. He was seconds away from throwing reason and common sense out the window.

When Garrett didn't move, he sat up and slowly moved away. Garrett got up, picked up his clothes, and threw Aubrey his. He caught his pants and shirt. They were mostly dry, so he pulled them on, trying to ignore the slightly clammy feeling. His boots were another story, but he pulled them on anyway, and then they mounted their horses.

"Race you back," Garrett said and took off.

Aubrey whooped and kicked his horse to let her know she had free rein. The speed sent his much lighter heart racing faster than his horse pounded the ground. There was a way out of the thorny trail he was on. Now he just had to stick to it, and he could have what he wanted—at least most of what he wanted. As long as the rug wasn't pulled from under him again.

As he reined to a stop in the yard, grinning and breathless, he realized the number of balls he was juggling might have decreased for the first time.

Chapter Twelve

"ARE you sure?" Barry asked as Aubrey stood in his cramped office in the back of the club. "You're the most popular dancer I have." He turned slightly green. "Guys come from all over to see you."

"That may be true, but next week is my last show. This isn't what I want to do with my life, and you know that. I took this job because I needed money desperately. Well, I've found something… someone I need more." He wanted to try to explain what the job was doing to him, but every time he tried, it sounded condescending and wrong in his head, so he skipped that part.

"Okay. I understand." Barry shrugged, most likely trying to cover for his disappointment. "There isn't anything I can do to change your mind?"

"No. I appreciate everything you've done and all you've taught me."

Barry shook his head. "Kid, you taught me." He leaned back in his chair with a smile. "We used to do this normal 'take it off' show. You added the whole Lone Rancher bit, and then all the other guys wanted an act too. Now we pack them in and have to turn guys away on the weekends because we can't fit them in the place. I've got you to thank for that."

"What will you do going forward?" Aubrey asked.

"Don't know yet. But I'll have to search for a new persona." He puffed his chest out, and Aubrey shook his head.

"You need to continue to rein in this potential train wreck. Find some new blood. Maybe someone who can do a Phantom of the Opera type bit. Different mask, different music, hidden identity. I really think that was what kept them curious." Aubrey turned to leave the office.

"Hey," Barry said to stop him. "If you change your mind… or something changes… let me know."

"I will." Aubrey pulled open the door and left the office, heading to the changing room next door to get ready for the first show.

Half-naked guys talked over each other as they dressed. Aubrey was running late, so he hurried to get into his outfit. He was going on right at the start of the show and then again toward the end. Aubrey figured that since these were his last few shows, Barry wanted to get the most from him that he could. Not that it really mattered. He'd be done after next week, and his heart and spirit felt as light as a feather. That alone told him that he'd done the right thing.

"Ten minutes," Barry called, and they all went into high gear, checking costumes and their reflections in the mirror before their first appearance of the night.

Aubrey went to stand in the wings, watching the crowd and waiting for his entrance. He always checked now to see if there were any familiar faces, one in particular, that he hoped he never saw out front. He knew each week he was taking a chance. The mask wouldn't be enough to hide from Garrett. They had seen each other's bodies, and Aubrey knew he wouldn't need to see Garrett's face to know him, and he assumed the same was true—that Garrett would know him, mask or not.

When it was his turn, Aubrey danced like he'd never danced before. He had energy, and he felt on top of the moon. The crowd roared their approval and excitement. Unlike the way things had been for weeks, he felt their approval and fed on it, jumping farther and kicking higher. By the time he was done, standing on the edge of the stage in his mask, boots, hat, and thong, he barely registered what he'd been doing. His entire body was alive and singing, not because of the dancing, but because his heart was light and he could simply enjoy what he was doing. The end was in sight, and all he saw behind the crowd of people was the lure of home. Three more shows and this part of his life would be over. Then, hopefully, his real life, the one he wanted deep down in his heart, could finally begin.

Aubrey worked his way through the crowd, feet barely touching the floor. A man slipped him a twenty, and Aubrey caressed his cheek. Another pressed some bills into his string, and Aubrey accepted the pat on the butt with a smile and a wiggle. It wasn't as though they were really touching him. Somehow in the last hour a bubble had formed around him, and no matter what they did, he felt nothing.

When his music ended, Aubrey bounded to the stage, waved his hat, and gave them all a cowboy yell, gyrating his hips. More bills came his way, and one of the security guys picked them up for him. With a final wave, Aubrey ran off the stage and sat down in a chair, breathing deeply.

"Did you leave anything for us?" one of the dancers groused as he got ready to go on stage. Aubrey didn't look up. He needed to breathe. Fletcher, one of the security guards, handed him the cash that had been thrown on the stage.

"Thanks," Aubrey said.

"I've been watching your show for months, and that was the best ever. What happened?"

Aubrey met his dark eyes. Under normal circumstances, Fletcher would be the kind of guy he could go for, but he barely noticed anything beyond his eyes. "I fell in love," he answered honestly before he could stop. The sentiment came out, and he'd said the words, the ones he'd been holding close to his heart. Then it hit him—he hadn't said them to the person he should have.

"So you were dancing for him. Was he out front? And did whatever you were trying to do work?"

"No. Thankfully he wasn't out front, and I guess I was dancing for someone I never have before."

Fletcher tilted his head slightly.

"I guess I was dancing for me," Aubrey said.

Fletcher left without another word, and Aubrey wondered what that meant. Maybe Fletcher had his answer, and that was all he wanted. Aubrey dressed for the second show, and then Fletcher returned. "I don't understand."

"What?"

"Why were you dancing for you?" Fletcher asked.

Aubrey fastened the Velcro on his tearaway jeans. "Does it matter, really?" The earnestness in Fletcher's eyes told him it did.

"Why weren't you dancing for him?"

"Because he doesn't know." Aubrey shifted to the edge of his seat. "I took this job because I had to… for the money. And that's why I did it. The exact reasons aren't really important. But tonight I danced for me. I can be happy in what I'm doing because it's almost over." There was some truth in the fact that sometimes talking to a stranger was easier than talking to someone you knew. "See, I was dancing because soon I can go home and stop living this part of my life."

"Is it true that no one knows who you really are?"

"Yeah," Aubrey answered, and then Fletcher got called away. Aubrey returned to making sure his costume was ready for the last show. It would be late when it was over. He had his hotel, but all he wanted was to get in his car and drive home. He'd call the hotel and tell them that he wasn't coming. Then he'd get home and rest so he could go find Garrett and tell him what he'd realized and what he deserved to hear.

The time ticked by quickly, but Aubrey barely felt it pass. All he wanted was for this show to be over. The sooner it was, the quicker he'd see Garrett.

Now that he knew how he felt, that bubble he'd been in for the first show seemed to thicken. This wasn't him. It was a character he was playing. The Lone Rancher might be up on stage, but Aubrey was in love with Garrett and wanted to get home as quickly as possible.

"Ladies, gentlemen, and those of you who have yet to make up their minds…." Barry's introduction reached his ears.

Aubrey's heart raced, not with excitement about his dance, but with anticipation of having this night over so he could go home.

"That's right, the man you've all been waiting for. He's young, hot, and he knows the meaning of save a horse, ride a cowboy. Hi-ho stripper! Away!"

The crowd yelled and whistled, but Aubrey heard little of it. His mind and attention were on a man back home. He just had to get through the next few hours, and then only one more night of dancing next week. He was so tired of this juggling act.

"The one and only Lone Rancher," Barry called, and Aubrey ran out onto the stage and began his dance. The lights were dang near blinding, and the energy in the room was electric. All he had to do was get through this show, and he could go back to Garrett. The music thrummed, and his vision filled with Garrett's eyes. In fact, everyone in the audience he could see had those same eyes. Even though Garrett wasn't there, he was still dancing for him.

His first number ended, and the trumpet fanfare began. The entire place erupted as the gallop portion of the *William Tell* Overture began to play. He hammed it up, playing to the crowd, throwing his hat offstage and then his shirt, after twirling it over his head. Through the din, a small commotion started in the back, but it quickly died down. Aubrey had learned long ago not to let anything distract him, so as the music built he went into his gallop routine, the fringe on his chaps slapping his legs before they were ripped away, leaving him in only his jeans, mask, and boots.

As the music came to its climax, Aubrey ground his hips, reached for the tops of his pants, and pulled them away, revealing a saddle-leather-colored thong that sent the entire club into an uproar.

Aubrey came to a stop at the edge of the stage as the last notes of music came to an end, replaced by slightly softer western music, which was his cue to head out into the crowd to play for tips.

The lights shifted so Aubrey could see the stairs. He checked where he was going and then scanned the crowd to decide where he should go first. Guys waved their money, yelling, shouting, and hooting at the top of their lungs. However, above all that his ears picked up a still portion of the room. Aubrey turned in that direction to see what was wrong and stopped dead in his tracks.

His mother stood off to his left, her purse clutched in front of her like a shield. Even from there he could see her wide eyes and open mouth. He locked gazes with her and knew instantly that no mask would ever hide his identity from her, not in a million years.

Aubrey was glued to the stairs, unable to move. His mother turned away, and then he saw Garrett. No surprise on his face—only deep and abiding pain.

He was suddenly frigidly cold and more exposed than he'd ever felt in his life. Forcing his legs to work, he took the few steps to the floor, intent on hurrying over to them, but as the crowd closed around him, hands reaching out, he saw Garrett turn and disappear. He made his way to where they'd been, but neither Garrett nor his mother were anywhere to be found. Aubrey wanted to get the hell out of there, but there was only one way out, back through the crowd, so he made his pass as quickly as he could before waving to the crowd and ducking backstage.

Aubrey didn't stop until he'd reached the bathroom.
He managed to push the door closed and reach the
stall before he lost the contents of his stomach. Once
he could straighten up and had rinsed his mouth, he
wondered what in the hell he was going to do and if he
had a home to go back to. God, the look on both their
faces had told him everything he could possibly have
wanted to know.

His mother and Garrett, both of them here tonight,
and they'd seen him. There was no hiding now. The
thought nearly sent him back to the bathroom, but he
steadied his breathing and somehow managed to quell
the panic attack that threatened to overtake him.

"What the hell happened?" Barry barked as soon
as Aubrey closed the bathroom door.

"My mother was out front."

"That was the old lady who…. Shit. I take it she's
the reason you wear the mask." Barry didn't wait for
an answer. "That's a tough break." He shook his head,
commiserating for thirty seconds. "The show has to
go on, kid. No matter what. So get ready for the last
number and then you can take off."

"How am I supposed to do that?"

Barry looked him over from head to toe. "Cowboy
up." Then he turned, leaving Aubrey alone.

Chapter Thirteen

AUBREY left the club as soon as he could break away and headed right for his hotel. With any luck Garrett would bring his mother there, knowing where he usually stayed. Maybe they could have out whatever was going to happen…. Lord, Aubrey's thoughts were as scattered as his driving. He pulled off the road after going a few blocks, breathing heavily and hoping like hell he didn't throw up again.

What little he had left in his stomach stayed there, and he pulled back on the road, concentrating until he pulled into the hotel and made a loop of the parking lot. There were no familiar vehicles, just the anonymous ones of the various other strangers who were staying there. Aubrey pulled into a space and stared straight ahead out the window, the engine off, cab quickly heating, glass fogging, but he didn't really see any of it. All he could think about was the fact that his secret was out and he'd seen the faces of his mother and Garrett.

His mother's expression seemed somewhere between "I never want to see you again for the rest of my life" and "I don't care how old you are, when we get home, I'm going to get the belt" anger. The shock, the temper, the way her lips curled in disgust, all of it played before his eyes. It didn't matter how hot the night was, that had been enough to send ice cubes running through his veins, prickling at him from the inside. The cold was there no matter what, a raging itch where there was no way he could get at it.

He tried to force his mind's eye away from his mother, but Garrett came into brilliant focus instead. The anguish he'd seen in his eyes had been enough to rip his heart in two. When he'd raced for the bathroom, it hadn't been his mother's chilling rage that had sent him running. It was the haunted disappointment and the way the light that he'd seen in Garrett's eyes when he looked at him had dimmed out right in front of him, like someone had taken a hood and snuffed out the one light that had colored his life. Only darkness loomed, without anything ahead to guide the way.

That was it, a tunnel. He was in a tunnel with no lights and only the vaguest idea of how long it was. He was alone, and one false move would send him crashing into the sides. The thing was—and this was the real kicker—he knew he'd been the one to construct it. The tunnel was of his own making, and he had to navigate and deal with his own creation. All of this was his fault, and his alone. He'd thought he could manage to keep everything in the air, and now it had all come crashing down around him.

Aubrey got out of the truck. He caught a glimpse of himself in the mirror and realized he was still wearing his stupid mask. He swore under his breath and ripped the ridiculous scrap of fabric off his face and threw it to the ground. Then he kicked it, sending the fabric upward where the breeze held it aloft for a few moments before sending it fluttering back to the ground. Aubrey watched it and then turned. He grabbed his bag from behind the seat, then snatched up the mask and shoved it in the bag before marching into the hotel.

He checked in and went to his room, placing his phone next to the bed. He looked at the display, hoping there had been a call or a message he'd somehow missed in the last ten minutes since he'd checked it and found the exact same result. No messages, no calls. Silence. Aubrey thought of calling either of them, but frankly, he was too afraid to. He sat on the edge of the bed, staring at his phone and holding his head, lost in misery. He wasn't sure what he should do next. But knowing that worrying wasn't going to change anything, he stood, cleaned up, and decided he might as well try to get some sleep.

Aubrey had just turned out the light and tried to close his eyes when his phone chimed. He yanked it off the nightstand and saw a text from Garrett. His stomach did a little roll until he looked at the text.

I took your mother home. That was all it said. He answered it, thanking Garrett, then waited for a reply but got nothing at all.

AUBREY gave up trying to sleep when the first light of dawn broke through his windows. He might have been better off sticking with his original plan and just gone on home, but he hadn't wanted a huge fight in the middle of the night. He had thought maybe a few hours' distance would help him think. He was so wrong. All he'd done was spend the entire night wondering if he'd have a home to go back to.

Rather than put it off any longer, Aubrey got out of bed, showered, and packed up his things. Then he left the hotel, checked his phone, as was quickly becoming his habit, and got into the truck.

The drive was both fast and slow at the same time. In a way, Aubrey couldn't get back fast enough so he could try to explain to his parents, and especially his mother, why he'd been doing what he was doing. But the thought of getting there and finding out he didn't have a home, the boyfriend he'd hoped for—and God, the fact that everyone in town was going to know his business—scared him half to death. What the hell was his father going to think, or his friends? Aubrey thought about calling Carolann, but it was too early in the morning. Maybe if the worst happened, he could go stay with her for a while.

Eventually the distance between him and the ranch closed, and Aubrey pulled into the drive, stopping in his usual spot near the house. He got out and looked around, half expecting the ranch to feel different. But it looked the same, and he noted that he'd need to paint the house soon. Everything smelled the same—horses, cattle, hay, spiced with a touch of manure, and the earthy, down-home scent of the land. Aubrey left his case where it was and went right into the barn. Maybe some hard work would give him some insight into what he should do. He grabbed a shovel and a wheelbarrow and started in to work.

"Boy!" his father called, voice echoing through the barn.

Aubrey wiped his brow and set his shovel aside. "Yeah, Dad, I'm back here."

"You better come out so we can talk," his father said almost flatly, as though he was trying to keep his temper under control.

Aubrey knew that was bad. When his father got angry, he usually let it out and then went on. Opening the stall door, Aubrey paused.

"What are you waiting for?" his dad said.

Aubrey hadn't heard that tone since he smashed the truck. Fuck it. He stepped out, closed the stall door behind him, and stared at his father. They each stood at one end of the barn, glaring at each other like they were gunfighters in the Old West.

"Your mother and I have been up half the night. Mostly that woman has been crying because what she saw broke her heart." His father crossed his arms over his chest. "All I have to ask you is, what do you have to say for yourself?"

Aubrey took a deep breath, sighed a few times, and then shook his head. "What do you want me to say, Dad? As you told me before, I'm an adult, and I told you I wasn't doing anything illegal. I never lied…."

"The hell you didn't. There are many fucking kinds of lies that a man can tell, and blatantly leaving out the important parts about the kind of man you are sure as hell is lying." He took a couple steps closer, but Aubrey held his ground. "I understand the—" His father swallowed. "—the dancing thing. At least I think I do. That's how you paid off all them bills, isn't it?"

Aubrey nodded. "I've been doing it for months. Didn't much care for it, if you want to know the truth."

"So you did it for the money?" His father sighed, and his eyes showed only relief. "You did this dancing and took your clothes off for the money so you could pay down the debts your mom and I owed." His dad wobbled a little bit, and Aubrey rushed forward, propping his father up and helping him to a bale of hay. "All this was about the money," he muttered.

Aubrey didn't say anything, making sure his dad got seated and off his feet.

"We were up all night, your mom crying about how she found you in a place like that."

"I would have talked to her, Dad."

He patted Aubrey's hand. "I know, son. And I now realize that you were only doing what you had to in order to pay for our mistakes." He leaned back against the stall wall. "To think we drove you to work in a place like that… to do what you did in front of a bunch of…." His dad clamped his eyes closed. "Your mother will be relieved that you… well, that you did it for the money."

Aubrey nodded, and then the realization of what his father was saying slammed into him. "Wait, Dad."

"What is it, son?" When his eyes slid open, Aubrey thought his dad seemed fragile all of a sudden.

Aubrey looked around and grabbed another bale, setting it across from his father. Then he took a seat. "I've done a lot of things. Some have been the wrong things, at least in your mind, but I tried to do them for the right reasons." Aubrey watched his father's eyes. "And there are things I should have told you and Mom a long time ago." His father's eyes darkened. "See, Dad, I should have trusted you, but I didn't."

"Excuse me?" his father said.

"Dad, I should have trusted you and Mom, in the way you love me." Aubrey couldn't get anything out above a whisper. "You and Mom always made sure Carolann and I had whatever we needed. You gave us horses and land where we could ride them. Yeah, we had to work hard, because that's what a ranch takes, but you gave us a lot, more than a lot of kids ever had."

"What are you trying to tell me, that you were working in that club because you're…." His father screwed up his lips, but nothing came out at first. "That way?"

"Dad, I worked in the club as a dancer so I could pay off the ranch debts. It wasn't something I'm proud of or expected to enjoy, but I was good at it." He realized that wasn't going to help make the point he needed to. "Dad, the thing is, I should have told you I was gay a while ago. I shouldn't have kept it from you."

His father glared at him, raised his hand, and pointed at him. "No, you should not."

"But I wasn't sure how you would feel."

His father sat up straight. "What the fuck does it matter what in the hell I feel?" He slowly got to his feet. "I gotta ask. Is being gay something that you chose? Did you wake up one morning and think that you were going to like men instead of women?"

"Of course not. It's part of who I am. Has been as long as I can remember." This had to be the hardest and most confusing conversation he'd ever had with anyone.

"So why in the hell are you apologizing to me for it?" his dad demanded. Aubrey blinked rapidly, trying to make sure he heard right. "I may have grown up in the middle of nowhere, and I may talk slow, but that doesn't mean I'm stupid. I've seen things on television, I watched *Will and Grace*, once. Maybe."

Aubrey nearly fell over he was so shocked. "I thought…."

"I know what you were thinking. This town isn't the most accepting place on God's green earth, but the people here are good people, and if you give them a chance, most of them will come to understand, or at least they'll try." He looked toward the house. "Your mother, on the other hand, is not one of those people." His father sat back down. "Look, son, your sister isn't showing any signs of getting close to settling down with anyone. And your mother wants a grandchild so badly she can taste it. You were her last chance."

"I can't live my life for anyone else," Aubrey said.

"I know that, son. The problem is that by not telling us who you really were, you have been living for us and for her. Rational or not, right or not, your mother had expectations that were ripped away from her last night."

"So it's not that I'm gay…."

"Your mother was raised, just like me, with old-fashioned values, and she's having a real hard time with this."

"I should go talk to her," Aubrey said, but his father reached out, smacking him lightly on the side of the head.

"Are you crazy? She knows you're home and is staying in the house. You do your work and stay away from her."

"Huh?"

"She needs to come to you." He held Aubrey's gaze in a steel vise. "I love your momma with every ounce of my being. She knows me better than anyone alive, and she doesn't think I notice a thing, but I do." He smiled in a way that Aubrey couldn't read. "She's a proud woman, and she likes to get her own way. If she doesn't get it the first time, she's usually trying to figure out a way to get it later. Not that she wants all that much most of the time, but Lord…." He pulled off his hat and wiped his brow. "This is a fight she can't win. Not if you want to have a life of your own. She has her heart set on grandchildren and a daughter-in-law."

"I will not marry to please her."

"Not saying you should." He shook his head hard. "But she won't see it that way."

Aubrey nodded and turned to go back to work. He didn't hear his dad move, and at the stall door he turned once again. His dad stood in place, staring at him intently. He closed his eyes and waited for the other shoe to drop. He half expected this to be the point where his father said the headaches weren't worth it and it would be best if Aubrey simply left. "What is it?" he asked when he couldn't take the staring any longer.

"I… I don't want you to think I really understand this, because I don't." This had been the reaction he'd expected from his father. "I love your mother, and I don't think I could ever be happy without her."

"Yeah?" Aubrey prompted. "If you want me to leave, then…."

"Hush, I never said that. I'm just being honest. I don't understand, but that don't mean I won't try." He put his hands on his hips, continuing to stare.

"Then what's going on?"

"I keep wondering what's different, and I don't see nothing," his dad finally admitted.

"Because nothing is different. I haven't changed. I'm still your son, and I'm still the person who loves working here on the ranch. And I'm still the guy you can count on to run the ranch and take care of you and Mom. I'm still me."

"But…."

"Dad, as you said earlier, I've always been gay. The only difference is that you know it now." And the fact that the secret he'd held to himself all these years was out in the open. So maybe he was different. The weight he'd been carrying was gone. The release of that weight had come with a price, and he'd yet to learn how much that price would be, but it looked like his father was going to be okay.

"I suppose," his dad said. "It just seems strange that the first gay person I've actually met is my own son."

"That's not true, Dad. I'm sure you've met, talked with, and even done business with other gay people. You just didn't know it." Aubrey went inside the stall and got to work. Eventually he heard his father leave the barn, and he settled into his work routine.

Even though his body felt better for the physical activity, his heart ached, and he longed to call Garrett. At one point his phone dinged with a message, and he jumped to check. It was his dad to say he should stay out there a little while longer, which was fine with him. The last thing he wanted was to take on his mother when she was on a tear, especially if he was the source of her exasperation.

Finally, as the morning heat began to build, Aubrey put the horses out in their paddocks and figured he might as well check on the cattle. He walked to the new tractor and started the engine. He was backing it out of the shed when he saw his mother step behind him. Aubrey slammed on the brakes to stop the machine. "Do you want me to run you over?" Aubrey asked, more harshly than he intended.

"So you do still care about your mother," she countered.

"Of course I do," Aubrey said.

"Then what in the hell was all that last night? Have you been doing—" She waved her arms in some imitation of his dance moves. If she hadn't been so angry, he might have laughed, but that would only make matters worse. "*That*," she spat, "every time you went to Dallas to see these *friends* of yours? Are they the ones who got you caught up in that mess?" She yelled all of that over the tractor engine until Aubrey turned it off. Then the silence seemed to reverberate off the walls as she glared at him.

"Mom, I danced to pay off the debts so I could save the ranch. The credit cards, the mortgage, even the down payment on this… that money came from that job." He kept his voice gentle but firm.

"So your leading a life of sin is my fault."

"I had to get money quickly, and when I was in Dallas once, months ago, I found out about a job that would pay a grand a night. I thought the guy was insane, but it turned out to be true."

She placed her hands on her hips. "Did you whore yourself out?"

"No," Aubrey snapped and climbed down from the seat, feeling more vulnerable now that there wasn't a tractor between them. "It was a job, and I did what I had to so you could stay in your home." His temper was hanging by a thread.

"Taking your clothes off in front of perverts and shaking what the good Lord gave you to make money." The way her lip curled had Aubrey seeing red. "I know what goes on in places like that."

"You do? How?" Aubrey challenged. "Sounds to me as though you've been sitting in your ivory tower passing judgment." He unclenched the fists he hadn't realized he'd made.

"Don't talk back to me."

"I'm arguing with you, and I'm not a child. I'm a man, and I have my own life. And I'll make my own decisions. I'm not happy about how you found out, but now you know I'm gay."

"You are not!" Defiance filled her eyes.

"Yes, Mom, I am," he said gently. "And no amount of wishing or anger on your part is going to change that. I am who I am, and I know I'm a disappointment to you, but facts are facts."

"Under my roof…," she began but stopped dead in her tracks. Her eyes softened, and Aubrey watched as her hands clenched into fists and then released. He was so his mother's son.

Aubrey stood and waited, careful to say nothing that couldn't be unsaid. His mother raised herself to her full height, still staring points of fire. Then, like a whirlwind, she turned on her heels and walked straight back toward the house. Aubrey stood where he was, staring after her, wondering if he'd gotten his point across or not. Hell, he wanted to know why she'd followed him with Garrett and whose idea that little scheme had been. Not that it really mattered; the end result was the same.

He climbed back on the tractor and started the engine, pulled out of the shed and into the yard, and turned around carefully before heading out. As he did, he saw his mother standing on the porch, scowling at him. Aubrey debated whether he should stop or just continue on, but making her angrier wouldn't help anyone.

"Yeah, Mom?" he said, leaning out the window.

"Come in and eat before you go out." She went right back inside, letting the door snap closed after her.

Aubrey shook his head and turned off the engine, then climbed down from the tractor to do as she wanted.

NO one said a damn word at breakfast. Aubrey's mother glared at him as she ate, and his dad rolled his eyes once and paid no attention to either of them. If she kept that up for much longer, there wouldn't be any need for air-conditioning in the house. Once Aubrey was done, he left and headed out to work.

He got the tractor running again, lifted a round bale of hay onto the fork in front, and carried it with him as he went in search of the herd.

He found them after about fifteen minutes and dropped the hay to supplement the grass and wondered what else he could do to pass the day. Going back to face his mother was about as enticing as poison ivy in his underwear. There were always chores to do, but he wasn't in the mood. His thoughts kept running back to Garrett and the betrayal on his face.

He turned the tractor toward the neighboring ranch on the slim chance he'd see Garrett. Of course, as he approached the fence line, all he saw were cattle dotting the landscape and rolling grassland as far as the eye could see.

"I really fucked up," Aubrey said under his breath. He pulled out his phone, but the signal was weak, fading in and out. Giving up, he shoved it back into his pocket and turned the tractor toward home.

The ride back was the same as the ride out, and he pulled into the yard and drove the tractor back into the shed before turning off the engine. His sweaty shirt stuck to the seat when he got down, and Aubrey pulled it over his head, carrying it as he closed the shed door and then approached the front of the house.

Garrett's truck was parked next to his dad's. Aubrey picked up his pace and pulled the door open, hurrying inside. "Is Garrett here?" he asked his dad with more excitement than was warranted if he wanted to keep things with Garrett a secret.

"Somewhere. Your mother called him."

Aubrey raised his eyebrows.

"I think after they both found you last night, they've developed some sort of bond or something. Like war buddies." He grinned, and Aubrey shook his head. Sometimes he still didn't get his father's sense of humor.

"Okay, Dad," he said sarcastically.

"Last night was a shock for your mother. I don't think she saw that coming in any way. Her image of you was blown all to hell." His dad raised his hand when Aubrey opened his mouth. "I'm not saying she didn't need to know, or that you being gay is a bad thing. But put yourself in her shoes. She learned her son was gay by finding out he was the entertainment in a strip club. That'd be pretty shocking to anyone."

"I know," Aubrey breathed.

His dad settled back in his chair. "I'm only glad I wasn't there. Knowing you're gay is one thing, but seeing it is quite another." He pushed the footrest up and turned to the television. "Son, I love you, but please make sure I never have to see… anything. You know what I mean."

"So I can be gay, but you don't want to know about it or be part of my life."

He flopped the chair upright in a single motion. "I didn't say that. Just that I don't want to see any…

you know… sex stuff. Or naked stuff. Any more than you would want to see stuff like that with your mother and me."

Aubrey took a step back, shivering. "Point taken."

He heard his mother come inside and then leave again, so he followed her out to her vegetable garden where he found Garrett bent over, picking what looked like peppers. Aubrey stood still, watching Garrett. His mother set the basket she'd gotten on the ground and began picking as well.

"I can't get my head around last night," his mother was saying. "He told me today that he was gay, and that he was dancing only for the money." She wiped her brow. "I don't want to say he's lying…."

"Then don't," Garrett said.

"I wasn't," Aubrey added as he strode toward them. "I've never lied to either one of you. Yes, I may not have told you all that I was doing, but I didn't lie, and I never cheated on anyone." Aubrey looked straight at Garrett, willing him to understand. "Mom and Dad were going to lose the ranch. I needed money, and I could dance. So I took the job to make what I needed. I had already told the manager I was going to be done next week." He knew he was pleading.

"I asked Garrett to come over to get some peppers for his folks, not so you could bare your soul," his mother snapped. "Why would Garrett care why you did what you did? I thought there was something fishy with all this travel to Dallas, and I asked him to drive me down."

"How did you find me?" Aubrey asked, still looking at Garrett, pleading with his eyes.

"We followed you," Garrett said. "We saw you go into the club and thought we must have been crazy and that you'd come right out. But you didn't. We found out there were two shows and debated going in. By the time we'd decided, they had closed the doors, so we got some dinner and then went to the second one." Garrett shook his head. "I can't believe that was you."

"It was."

"I talked to you outside in the alley. You knew who I was then. And you said you didn't meet with guys on the side. Was that because you knew who I was?"

"Of course not. I never went with guys at the club. I danced, nothing more." He glanced at his mother, heart racing. "I only danced for the money, to save the ranch."

His mother was looking at them, alternating back and forth like she was watching a tennis match. Aubrey saw her becoming more and more confused.

"I was so disappointed because I'd liked you for a while," Aubrey said, "but you seemed interested in the dancers. I thought you'd gone out with Simon."

"Please. I was interested in you because you looked like this friend from back home, and I thought I could have some fun with you because I couldn't with him. Turned out it was the same person all along." Garrett bent down and picked up the paper bag he'd been picking into.

"Garrett…," Aubrey breathed, needing to try to hold on to what he desperately wanted.

"I need some time," Garrett said. "Thanks, Mrs. Klein, for the peppers." He turned and strode away fast but without breaking into a run.

Aubrey stared after him, his heart aching with each step Garrett took.

"He's your friend. He'll forgive you." His mother gathered up what she'd been picking.

"Mom," Aubrey said. "Don't you get it? Garrett went to the club as a patron."

She blinked at him, and then the basket she'd been holding tumbled to the ground. "He's...." Comprehension shone in her eyes.

"We've been dating, Mom," Aubrey said with a small sigh. "I like him." He didn't look away from the place where Garrett had disappeared around the corner of the house. "I know you don't want to hear this, but when I was growing up, you always said that what you wanted most was for us to be happy. Well, Garrett makes me happy. Or at least he did." Aubrey knelt down and gathered the peppers back into the basket, then handed it to her. "I wish you could have left things well enough alone. I was almost done with the dancing and had made the money we needed to get the ranch back on track."

"I thought you were maybe seeing someone, or...."

"You thought I might have been seeing a woman?"

"I didn't know what to think. The trips to Dallas started to seem suspicious to me, so I asked Garrett to drive me down. I guess they must have seemed the same to him, because he took me. I had no idea what I'd find. You—"

"I'm an adult, Mother, and as such I am entitled to make my own decisions." He wanted to yell at her, but that wouldn't do any good, and she was still his momma. He loved her, but he was so frustrated with her too. "You won't always agree with them, and that's fine, but I did what I did to help you and Dad. I didn't max out the credit cards or overextend the ranch's credit. I just came home and found out how close you were to losing this place, and when the job was offered when I was visiting Dallas, I took it because we needed the money."

She wasn't going to give up, not for a second. "But that?"

"Is it that I was dancing that bothers you? That I'm gay? All of it?" Aubrey asked. "Because none of that can be changed. I like men, not women, and I'm still your son, the one who swallowed his pride and dignity each and every week for months to make sure that you'd still have the home you love." Aubrey's head throbbed, and all he wanted was to take something and lie down. "I did what I had to. I wore the mask because I didn't want people to know who I was."

"Because you were ashamed. And why would you do something you were ashamed of? I raised you better than that." She stepped around him and started walking toward the house.

"You don't get it, Momma. I did all that for you. Every week, every show, all the money I got, I did it for you and Dad." She stopped in her tracks. She didn't turn around or move other than to lower her head. Her shoulders shook, and Aubrey groaned softly, hurrying to her. He put his arms around her. "I didn't mean to make you sad."

"But I did this," she said.

"No, Mom. You overspent, and I worked to try to save the ranch, but you didn't make me gay. That's how I was born."

She sniffled and wiped her eyes. "But I must have done something."

"No, Mom," Aubrey repeated. "I am who I am, and wasn't something that you fed me or anything in the way you changed my diapers that made me this way."

She smacked him on the shoulder. "Now you're being a smartass."

"No. I'm being truthful. I know it's hard for you to accept, and it may take you some time, but I did what I did to help the family. If I had to do it over again, I would, because you, Dad, and this ranch—our ranch—are worth it."

She stepped away and looked up into Aubrey's eyes. He could feel her searching for something, and then she nodded.

"I've always told you the truth, Mom."

"You never told me you were gay."

"No, I didn't. I wasn't ready to." Aubrey chuckled. "I'm still not sure I'm ready, but things are what they are."

"This is going to take me some time to work through."

"I know, Mom. I've had years to come to terms with who I am. I guess I can give you the time you need." He released her. "But you have to promise you won't try to fix me up with anyone."

She pulled open the back door. "Are you sure you just haven't met the right girl?"

"Yes, Mother," he answered flatly. "They don't have anything that interests me… you know, that way." God, this conversation was too much. "Just let me try to figure out my own love life." He wasn't sure she was going to give up. "Let me ask you," he said as he followed his mom inside. "Would it really be so bad if you had a son-in-law instead of a daughter-in-law?" He held her gaze, but she didn't answer.

Eventually Aubrey left the room. Talking didn't seem to be doing any good at this point. She had to come to terms with things in her own way. But on the whole, with his parents, anyhow, Aubrey figured he'd made out as well as could be expected. Now if only things with Garrett could find a way to work out as well. Unfortunately, Aubrey wasn't so sure there was a way for that to happen.

Aubrey smacked his hand on the table. He had to try, dammit. As Barry had told him when he'd been whining: *Cowboy up!* That was easy enough to say, and all Aubrey needed to do was figure out what in the heck he should do.

Chapter Fourteen

AUBREY worked. He wasn't sure what the hell else to do, so he worked, hard, for days. His muscles ached at the end of the day, during the night, and only calmed in the morning before he started over again. A lot of the chores he'd put off because he hadn't had time, like rebuilding the gate to the main paddock, were all done and dusted. This was a ranch, so the work never ended, but his list of things to do was getting small.

"Aubrey," his father called from outside the barn.

He stepped out of the last stall, inhaling the scent of fresh bedding that permeated the building. Nothing smelled better, in his opinion—well, except the way Garrett smelled after they'd been together, sweat, musk, and come all mixed together.

"What's wrong with you?" his dad asked, and Aubrey snapped out of the Garrett daze he'd been in. Not that it did him much good.

"Sorry," he answered softly.

"I need you to go into town. Howland's Supply called, and the fence posts you ordered are in and ready to be picked up. He said they'd help you load them if you can get there before noon. They have some extra help until then."

"Thanks, Dad," Aubrey said, already moving to put the tools away.

"Your head's been filled with cotton lately."

"I know. I've been preoccupied."

"About Garrett?" he asked. "Your mother told me what you said." His dad shrugged. "This is the one and only time I will ever say anything like this in my entire life." His dad shook his head and looked like he could hardly believe he was about to say anything now. "Garrett is a good man. I don't know nothing about being gay, but I know I want you happy, and if he'll make you happy, then go get him. Moping and pining around here like some teenager isn't going to get you what you want."

Aubrey blew out his breath. "I tried calling him, but he won't answer my calls." God, he sounded whiny, even to himself. "I think I should concentrate on the ranch and make sure everything here is done."

"Son, you gotta have a life that's more than the ranch." He shook his head once again. "Go on into town. Whatever chore you have set up for yourself will wait until you get back." He turned and left the barn, boots ringing on the concrete.

Aubrey put his tools and gloves away and pulled his shirt on over his head. Then he grabbed his hat

from the top of one of the stall posts and plopped it
onto his head.

The ride into town was fast, with little traffic. It gave
him time to think, which was exactly what he didn't need
more of. He parked in front of Howland's and went right
inside, dang near bumping into Garrett. Aubrey smiled,
and his heart did a little flippy thing in his chest. Garrett
stepped to the side without saying anything. Aubrey
stood his ground, meeting Garrett's gaze.

"You want something?" Garrett asked in a growly
whisper.

"Just to talk to you," Aubrey said, ignoring the tone.

"Aubrey, I've got your order ready."

"Thanks, Mr. Howland. I'll be right there." When
he turned back around, Garrett hurried past him
and out of the store. Aubrey did his best not to seem
disappointed and continued inside. Chasing Garrett
down on the street wasn't going to do him any good.

Aubrey paid for his order, and they got it loaded.
He thanked everyone for their help, promising to buy
the guys a beer the next time he saw them in town.
Then he pulled away and drove slowly, hoping to see
Garrett, but of course he didn't have that kind of luck.
Giving up, he headed out of town, back toward the
ranch, where he pulled into his spot near the barn.

The sun burned down, and the air was still and
hot as hell. He looked at the fencing in the back of the
truck and figured he could unload it later when it had
cooled off some, before the sun went down. He saddled
Marigold and led her out into the yard. His mother
stepped out onto the porch, and he waved to her. She
returned the gesture, and then he nudged Marigold
forward. Once away from the buildings, he let her pick
up speed, but he didn't want her to tax herself. She

wanted her head more than anything, but he kept her reined in and tried to enjoy the ride.

Once he reached the trees, he dismounted and led Marigold to the clearing. As soon as she was tied, he let her munch and settled on the log near the stream, watching the water as it trickled over the rocks.

"I know I screwed up," he said out loud, and Marigold huffed, lifting her head like she was listening. "I should have been honest with Garrett."

"Then why weren't you?"

Aubrey started as Garrett stepped through the trees, leading one of Bridger's horses. Aubrey stood and stared, blinking a few times, wondering why Garrett was here—happy that he was but still more than a little surprised. "I didn't think you'd understand."

"What? Being desperate enough for money to sell your pride and dignity? I understand that. Do you think I haven't done things that I'm not proud of?"

"I was hoping it would all be over and that I could put the whole thing behind me." Aubrey began speaking faster. "It was what I did for money. I never went home with anyone. You know that. I turned you down in the alley, just like I did any other guy who wanted more."

Garrett nodded and stepped closer. Aubrey sat back down on the old log, and Garrett eventually sat next to him. "Being able to trust the people in my life is important. Honesty is important," Garrett said.

"Yeah, I know." It was important to him too. "But every time I thought about telling you the truth, you'd say something about how straightforward I was."

"And you let me think that," Garrett countered angrily. "After I saw you in the club, I felt like such a fool. My parents only ever told me what they wanted me to know growing up. So anything that didn't fit what they believed they just left out of the discussion. Hell, when my grandmother passed away, they didn't tell me right away because they hadn't decided if they were going to go to the funeral because she didn't believe what they did." Garrett's eyes filled with tears, and Aubrey pretended not to see them even though he wanted to gather Garrett in his arms. He wanted to so badly his hands twitched, but he wasn't sure how Garrett would react. "See, my gran on my mother's side was a free spirit in the best sense of the word. I loved her to death, but my parents didn't let me visit her often because she might 'fill my head with her nonsense.'" Garrett did a pretty good imitation of his father. "They were always like that, so it hurts that you kept what you were doing from me."

"I don't know what to say," Aubrey said. "I did what I did to save the ranch."

Garrett stood and walked toward the water. "That's what pisses me off." Garrett turned back to face him. "You do this thing that I shouldn't be able to forgive you for, and fuck if you don't do it for a noble reason. It makes it damn near impossible to stay mad at you."

"Well, if you want to be angry, remember I outed you in front of my mother."

"Shit, yes." Garrett closed his eyes.

"If it helps, I doubt she'll say anything. Mom's having a hard time with me being gay. She isn't going to advertise it."

Garrett lifted his gaze and smiled. "Well, it was your mother who told me where you were."

Aubrey blinked and his jaw fell open. "My mother."

"Yeah. She said you and I needed to talk and that she was tired of seeing you mope around the ranch all the time. Then she said she'd be keeping an eye on me, and that I was to behave myself, whatever that means."

"It means she's trying," Aubrey said under his breath. "But I guess the real question is whether you are willing to give things a try… with me."

Garrett didn't give any indication of his thoughts, which was unnerving. "That depends."

"On what?"

"Are you going to be doing any more dancing?" Garrett asked.

"I'm supposed to do one last set of shows on Saturday. I gave my notice and told them they needed to replace me. But I promised I wouldn't leave them in the lurch." He felt like a complete heel. He wanted Garrett to take him back, and he needed more than anything to leave that part of his life behind. "I'll call and tell them that I'm done." He made the decision. "They know what happened with you and Mom, so Barry has to have an idea that I'm not going to be in."

"Is that what you want?" Garrett asked.

Aubrey reached up and pulled Garrett to him. "Yes. That's what I've wanted for quite some time as far as the dancing is concerned." He tugged Garrett even closer. "But if you're asking what my heart desires, that's pretty simple: horses, this ranch, and you. Not necessarily in that order."

"So, what exactly are you saying?" Garrett didn't come closer or move away.

"I'm saying that the next time the Lone Rancher makes an appearance, it will be behind a closed and locked door for a very private showing." He closed the gap between them, kissing Garrett hard.

"I wish you had told me," Garrett said when they parted.

"I should have. But it wasn't something I was proud of." Aubrey released Garrett. "Shame is a pretty debilitating thing. I never realized it before. I kept this whole part of my life a secret because I was ashamed of it."

"Do you mean the dancing?"

Aubrey shook his head. "All of it. I was ashamed of being gay and wanted to be like everyone else, so I kept it to myself. Then I went to Dallas, basically to get drunk after I found out how bad things were on the ranch, and I ended up wandering into the club. It was amateur night, and I'd had enough to drink that I got up on stage. They'd told me that was the way to get hired. I was pretty good and guys were throwing bills at me. When Barry saw it, he offered me the job, and I took it after seeing the money. He agreed that I could only dance the shows on Saturday, said things would get old otherwise… and I went from there." He felt a deep-seated need to explain everything to Garrett. He didn't want there to be anything else between them. "I wore the mask partly because I didn't want anyone who might see me to know who I was, but now I think it was because I was ashamed of who I was. It's what I hid behind. Yeah, I wore it at the club, but also at home. I hid who and what I was, and I'm not going to do that any longer. I have to be open and honest."

"But everyone will know."

"Then they know. I know now that lies breed lies, and shame only begets shame. Love can't exist with either, so I have to let them go."

Garrett began pacing the ground in front of him. "So you're not going to hide that you're gay?"

"Nope. Not going to broadcast it, either, but I won't hide who I am or the person I love." Aubrey stared at Garrett, who looked back at him. "I know now that I deserve to live without shame." Aubrey stood and walked to the edge of the trees, looking out over his family's ranchland. "Don't you?" he asked without turning around.

"Huh?" Garrett asked as he approached.

"I said, don't you deserve to live without shame running your life? We are who we are. Is the way I care for you ugly or disgusting?"

Garrett shook his head, pulled off his hat, and wiped his brow with the back of his hand. He set his hat on the log. "So you want to live openly?"

"Yeah."

"Where does that leave us?" Garrett asked.

"Where do you think?" Aubrey questioned right back. "I want to be open about how I feel about you, and I'm hoping you feel the same about me." He took a single step closer. "I know I hid stuff from you, but I would do just about anything to keep this land in my family. It's part of me, just like you are part of me."

Garrett blinked but stayed silent.

"Don't you know that I love you?" Aubrey asked. "Of course you don't, because I was never brave enough to say it before. But I do. I've cared about you for years, watched you, longed for you."

Garrett swallowed hard, his Adam's apple bobbing. "I wasn't sure, after…." He faltered and looked down at the ground. "I thought there was something special between us that night in the truck, but then all this happened, and you kept running away to Dallas all the time, so I thought I was some diversion, a little fun."

"Oh, you were fun, and hot, but you're way more than that. You stole my heart, and I was doing my best to try to hold on to it. I knew I was playing with fire with the dancing, but I had to save the ranch. Some things are worth more than my self-respect and my dignity, and the ranch is one of them. You are another." Aubrey hoped Garrett would understand why he did what he did and could find some way to forgive and get past it. Maybe it wasn't possible, and he would end up nursing a broken heart. The last few days had been hell, but he'd made it through, and he'd buck up and continue on if he had to. But he hoped....

"You really love me?" Garrett whispered.

Aubrey wasn't sure what he'd said at first. "Yes, I do. I should have told you that too. You deserved to hear it from me, and if you give me a chance, I'll make it a point to tell you... and show you what I feel. You were my friend growing up, and this ranch wouldn't be the same without you. I spent the past three days moping around because everywhere I looked I saw you. In the barn where we rode and played, right here where we swam. It's been you my whole life, and I never even realized it until I brought you home from the club, but by then I was in too deep to get out." Aubrey's hand quivered, and he shook it out hard, trying to get feeling back into it as he shifted his weight from foot to foot.

"How would this work?"

"I don't know, exactly. But it'll start with telling my folks about us. They already know or have an idea because of how useless I've been. After that, we'll have to figure things out between the two of us."

"My parents...."

"That's up to you. But word will get around to them." He knew there were pitfalls that looked to go halfway to China. "How we handle it is up to you. That is, assuming you want to...."

Garrett looked so far away that for a moment Aubrey wasn't sure he could reach him. "I'd rather walk through a pit of snakes than have that conversation with my mother and father. But I know I have to. There's been way too much hiding, from both of us."

"So...."

Garrett walked right up to him, pulling Aubrey into a tight embrace. "You had my heart that night you cared enough to take me in and bring me home." Garrett cradled Aubrey's cheeks in his hands, brown eyes as deep and mysterious as an abandoned mine shaft, boring into his. "I love you too." Garrett stilled.

"What is it?"

"I'm trying to think of the last time I told someone I loved them or I was told that I was loved, and I can't remember it at all."

"Not your mom and dad?"

"Maybe my mom, a long time ago, but never my father. He was always too stoic. Strange coming from a man who's supposed to believe in God's love surrounding and helping everyone, but it's true."

Aubrey brought his lips right to Garrett's. "Then let me say it again: I love you, Garrett, and I don't want to spend the rest of my life without you. Living with my mom and dad probably isn't the best situation, but we'll figure something out."

"Do you really think it's possible that we aren't going to get run out of town on a rail?"

"I've given it some thought. I know there will be people who won't like us. I may have to go farther for supplies and to sell the ranch's beef, but I can make it work. What I can't do is do it all alone. At least I don't want to." He closed his eyes for a second to let everything they'd talked about sink in. Garrett felt so amazing in his arms, and his heart soared as he let himself dream that he might get this each morning and every night. For that he'd work his ass off for the rest of his life. "The thing is—what do you want?"

"I want to be with you." Just like that, without batting an eyelash, Garrett answered and seemed to make his decision. "I'm tired of hiding who I am to make everyone happy when the only two who are important are you and me."

"So what do we do from here?" Aubrey asked.

Garrett reached for the hem of Aubrey's T-shirt, pulling it up and rubbing his belly. "I think we should cement our happiness with a little physical gratification."

"Out here?" Aubrey asked, slapping his arm. "I think we'll be eaten alive, and bugs are not something I want to worry about, especially with the goods on display."

Garrett chuckled and slowly pulled the fabric back into place. "Maybe we can go back to the ranch, get out of this heat, spend the afternoon watching sports on television, and at the end of the day, go into your room and close the door."

"Mom and Dad will know what we're doing," Aubrey said. "Besides, I want more than sex. I want to date, have fun, get to know one another, and really explore this. There's the old foreman's house, which would need some work, but we could fix it up and move in there. Mom and Dad would have their privacy, and we could have ours." He should have thought of that before. The place would need a lot of work, but it was something he and Garrett could do together. "I'll talk to Mom and Dad about it and make sure they're okay with the idea."

"What about my parents?"

"That's your decision. I'll stand by you whatever you decide to do, but you know they're going to get suspicious eventually."

"Then I'll tell them."

"What's the worst that could happen?" Aubrey said.

"They tell me to get out and have nothing more to do with me," Garrett answered.

"Is that something you can live with?" Aubrey asked quietly. That seemed like a heavy price to pay, and Aubrey was bone-deep afraid that Garrett would think he wasn't worth it. That they weren't worth it.

"I guess it is. My parents have wanted me to be something I'm not for so long I tend to think that's normal. But it isn't. Their expectations aren't mine, and it's time I live for myself." Aubrey could tell Garrett was a little afraid, but he kept that to himself. No man wanted to be reminded of his fears. "You're more important than they are, anyway. I think that was why the whole Lone Rancher thing hurt so much. You're important to me, and when I saw you up there, really saw you as you, I wondered if you were the same person I'd fallen in love with. I didn't think so for a while, but I know you are. I fell for the man who would do anything for the ones he loves, even sacrificing his dignity and pride to make sure they're safe. That's the man I love. You."

"Then let's go back." Aubrey pulled Garrett into a kiss that added to the heat of the day. "Maybe a little later. After all, it's really quiet out here." He tugged Garrett into another kiss, happy and contented. Garrett parted his lips, nibbling and sucking at Aubrey's. It was lovely and amazing. When Garrett moaned, Aubrey's heart raced faster and faster, and he didn't want to part for anything. But the heat and the whinny of the horses told them both it was time to go back.

Reluctantly, Aubrey released Garrett, who retrieved his hat, and they got their horses, mounted, and rode slowly back to the ranch. Aubrey made sure the horses were settled with plenty of water and hay before taking Garrett by the hand and leading him toward the house. Never before in his life had he even thought he'd be able to hold the hand, out in the open, of the person he loved. That simple act of open affection, extended and then returned, nearly overwhelmed him.

"Mom, Dad," Aubrey called when they stepped inside.

"We're in the kitchen," his mother answered, and he and Garrett took an initial step toward building a life together.

"There's something we need to talk about." Aubrey tightened his grip on Garrett's hand, and they stepped into the room. Aubrey noticed his father's gaze followed their hands. Though he was tempted to pull away, he held Garrett's hand tighter instead. It was quiet, and not a big deal in the grand scheme of things, but for them it was a statement.

"Sit on down. I have pie and there's tea." She didn't turn around, and Aubrey wondered if she was ignoring them, refusing to acknowledge what was happening, or didn't care. They released each other's hands, pulled out chairs, and sat down while his mother brought plates and glasses. "So was there something you wanted to talk about?"

"Well…," Aubrey began.

"Before we make a big brouhaha over anything," Aubrey's dad began, "we've decided that it would be best to leave the running and management of the ranch to you. I know you've been doing it for a while, but we wanted to make that official. We also want you to know that this is your home, and we know you're going to want to lead your own life."

Aubrey nodded and glanced at Garrett, wondering where this was going.

"You are an adult and perfectly capable of making your own decisions. Your mother and I have to accept that we aren't going to understand them all, but they are yours to make, and we will always be your parents, and you will always be our son."

"What does that mean, exactly?"

"That your father and I will accept and nurture your relationship the same as we would if you had brought home a woman."

Aubrey looked at each of them in turn, wondering where this sudden enlightenment had come from. "I appreciate that, but…." Aubrey's head was spinning.

"Your father and I spent a lot of time talking—"

"Last night and the night before," his dad interrupted.

His mother scowled briefly and then turned back to him. "There are plenty of things we don't understand in this world, and for now this is one of them. But you're our son, and that's what matters." She looked at his dad, who nodded. "So, Garrett, are you staying for dinner?"

"I…." He seemed at a loss for words, and Aubrey knew exactly how he felt. "That would be very nice. Thank you."

His mother left the kitchen. The three of them got up from the table and went into the living room. Aubrey thought he was going to be dizzy and sat on the sofa so he didn't fall over. Garrett sat next to him, and since the talking portion of the afternoon seemed to be over, his father turned up the volume on the television, and they all settled back to watch the Houston Astros get their bats handed to them. But it didn't matter. Aubrey held Garrett's hand, and at least here, in his home, they didn't have to hide.

"I think I just won the lottery," Aubrey whispered after a few minutes. Garrett didn't say anything, but the question in his eyes was more than enough. "I came through this, and in the end I got it all—the ranch, my family, and you." His father was engrossed in the program, so Aubrey leaned in close, nuzzling lightly behind Garrett's ear. "What more could I ask for?"

Epilogue

"**IF** they think I'm going to help with any of their activities, they have another think coming," Aubrey's mother said loudly enough she could probably be heard in Dallas. "And another thing, you tell her that she's one to talk after the way she acted. Miss High and Mighty, indeed." His momma was on a tear, and Aubrey knew well enough to stay away. "Yes, I know it's Easter, the time of renewal and forgiveness. Maybe that old bat should take a little of her own medicine before preaching to me or anyone else."

Aubrey turned to Garrett, who paled slightly. They both knew exactly who his mother was railing against.

"Tell her not to get involved. It isn't worth it," Garrett said sadly. "They aren't going to change their minds for any reason."

Aubrey stood and walked toward the kitchen. His mother was sitting at the table. "Why don't you tell her she can kiss my sweet, flower-scented behind? That woman is a menace, and its time her reign of self-righteousness comes to an end. So yes, I'm going to run for the head of the woman's auxiliary and then petition that she be removed from all boards for un-Christian behavior. Just because she's the deacon's wife doesn't mean she gets to run everything."

Aubrey turned and sat back down. "No way am I gonna stop her." When his mother got like this, and it had been happening quite a bit over the past six months, it was best to stay out of the way. Her righteous indignation was through the roof, and he wasn't about to get caught in her crossfire.

"My mother and father," Garrett began formally, "aren't going to change their minds about anything. Never have, and they won't start now."

The phone slammed into the cradle, ringing slightly, followed by muttering.

"Are you ready for lunch?" Aubrey's mother said.

Aubrey looked at Garrett, half tempted to answer that they had to go into town and would eat there just to get out of the house. "That would be nice," he said instead.

"You don't need to fight with my mother on my account," Garrett said.

Aubrey's mother tore into the room, stopping in front of Garrett, glaring at him for a split second, and then her expression softened. "Yes, I do. I know she's your momma, but that holier-than-thou act she's got going has my undies in a twist, and it's time it stopped. She doesn't own the church, and neither does your father."

"But…."

"Their behavior has been shameful," she countered, hands on her hips, daring either of them to contradict her. When neither did, she turned and went back into the kitchen. "Lunch in half an hour." A pan hit the stove with such force they both started slightly.

Garrett's mother and father hadn't spoken to him in months. Aubrey knew it had been what Garrett had feared, and while he'd said he was prepared for it before he'd come out to them, the actual rejection had hurt. It still did. Aubrey saw every ounce of pain in Garrett's eyes.

"I'm going out to the barn," Garrett said and went outside, the screen door banging closed behind him.

"Give him a few minutes," Aubrey's father said from his chair when Aubrey stood to go after him. "Sometimes a man needs to nurse his hurt on his own. He knows how we all feel, so leave him alone for now."

Aubrey sat back down, but his gaze kept traveling to the door. A steady stream of muttering came from the kitchen, renewed with Garrett's departure. After five minutes, Aubrey couldn't wait any longer and went outside, breathing in the sweet spring air as he strode across the yard. He found Garrett in one of the stalls, stroking Marigold's neck. "You know she's only being supportive."

"It isn't your mother." Garrett sighed. "What kind of person gets rejected by their own parents?"

Aubrey didn't answer because he'd already learned there was no good answer to that question. Garrett had asked it numerous times, and it was one of those things Aubrey knew Garrett had to answer for himself. However, when Garrett turned to him, Aubrey decided to break his silence. "It has nothing to do with you, and you know it. Your mom and dad made their decision, and they're the ones who have to live with that." Aubrey stepped inside the stall and tugged Garrett out, closing the door before pressing him against it, looking deeply into Garrett's chocolate-brown orbs.

"Doesn't mean I don't wish it were different."

"No. But the important question is, do you regret your decision?" Aubrey raised his eyebrows, and Garrett shook his head. "Then you made your choice, and so did they. I wish it was different too." He'd rather have a tooth pulled than put Garrett through what he was going through.

"I'll be okay. Sometimes it worries me how good your folks have been to me. Makes me wonder when it's going to end."

Aubrey wove his leg between Garrett's and wrapped his cowboy in his arms. "Momma is going to have lunch ready soon, and then we need to get the rest of our things moved out of the house." That brought a smile to Garrett's lips, just like Aubrey had hoped it would.

"Tonight we sleep in our own room in our own house."

"Yeah...." He leered darkly, and Garrett shivered, energy sparking between them, Garrett's erection pressing to Aubrey's hip as his own did the same. Living under the same roof with his folks had been harder than either of them had imagined. Not that his mom and dad were demanding. But Aubrey had found he was self-conscious. Now they could be as loud and athletic as they wanted.

Aubrey smiled and then closed the rest of the gap between them, sliding his lips over Garrett's, tasting his man while they rubbed their hips together. Aubrey cupped Garrett's bulge, rubbing slightly, Garrett shivered; clearly, they both wanted more.

"Lunch," his mother called with her usual impeccable timing. Garrett groaned, shaking a little in what Aubrey perceived as frustration that matched his own. Aubrey pulled away, and they went in to lunch.

MOVING the last of the things to the former foreman's house took the rest of the afternoon. Aubrey hadn't realized how much he'd accumulated until he had to move it. The house had been in worse shape than he'd originally thought, so it had taken longer than expected to get it ready for them.

The main room was large, with a fireplace. The furniture was just what they could pull together, but Aubrey was hoping that they could get new pieces soon. He had his eye on a set in saddle leather. The really important rooms were in better shape. The kitchen had been stocked by his mother, and the bedroom had everything they could need, including a queen-size bed and new bedding. They also had heavy forest-green curtains his mother had made that matched the spread she'd made them for Christmas.

"That's the last of it," Garrett said, bringing in a box and setting it in the bathroom. "Should I be scared you have this much stuff?" He pulled open the box. "Mousse?"

Aubrey cocked his head and didn't answer. A lot of that stuff had been from when he was dancing, and he should have thrown it out, but like other things, he'd only ended up collecting it and letting it sit. "I'll go through that later."

His phone rang, and Aubrey answered it. "Are you coming here for dinner?" his mother asked.

"No. We're all set and going to stay in," Aubrey answered.

"Okay." She was trying to keep her voice light, but Aubrey could tell she was disappointed.

"We'll see you tomorrow." Aubrey disconnected and sighed. The house was theirs, and they had a door they could lock and distance between them and his parents.

"I found this when I was unloading boxes from the back of the cab," Garrett said and dropped a fabric mask into his hand. Aubrey shook his head and was about to toss the mask into the trash when Garrett slinked into his arms. "Maybe we could resurrect the Lone Rancher one last time for a private show." Garrett took the mask and slid the elastic around Aubrey's head. "What do you think? I could hum the *William Tell* Overture for you."

Aubrey laughed outright, deep and throaty. "I gave all my tearaway pants to strippers in need."

"I can tear away your pants for you. Don't worry about that." Garrett sat on the edge of the bed expectantly. Aubrey grinned, shook his head, and slowly began to sway his hips to music he conjured up in his head. He felt a little silly, but Garrett's eyes darkened, and his mouth dropped open slightly. When Garrett leaned back, the prominent bulge told Aubrey all he needed to know. Aubrey added more movement, turning around to tug his shirt up. He twirled and pulled his shirt off the rest of the way, tossing it to Garrett, who sniffed it, smiled, and then rubbed it over his crotch.

Aubrey faltered a second when Garrett pulled off his belt and opened the top of his jeans, exposing a small V of warm flesh. He did the same, toeing off his shoes and then kicking them aside. Then he turned, giving Garrett a full view of his ass, swaying it back and forth. A groan, low and rumbly, told him he was having the effect he wanted.

There was no way to sexily take off pants he couldn't just tear off, but Aubrey managed it reasonably well, waving his bulging briefs as he shimmied closer and closer to Garrett, watching his partner's eyes round and his tongue wag as he got closer and closer.

"Fuck," Garrett breathed.

"Definitely," Aubrey whispered and began tugging off Garrett's shirt, rocking his hips like a metronome, watching as Garrett's eyes followed them back and forth. Garrett's shirt hit the floor, and he worked open his pants and then danced back. Aubrey turned and held on to the dresser, sticking his ass in Garrett's direction, waving it back and forth.

When he turned around, Garrett was naked, sitting back on the bed, motioning him over with his finger. *Ride 'em cowboy.*

Coming in March 2016

⟨ⓓ⟩REAMSPUN DESIRES

#5

Taylor Maid by Tara Lain

He'll marry the maid to get $50 million but a secret could queer the deal.

Taylor Fitzgerald needs a last-minute bride.

On the eve of his twenty-fifth birthday, the billionaire's son discovers that despite being gay, he must marry a woman before midnight or lose a fifty-million-dollar inheritance. So he hightails it to Las Vegas… where he meets the beautiful maid Ally May.

There's just one rather significant problem: Ally is actually Alessandro Macias, son of a tough Brazilian hotel magnate. But if Ally keeps pretending to be a girl for a little while longer, is there a chance they might discover this marriage is tailor made?

#6

Trial by Fire by BA Tortuga

One Aussie. One Texan. One baby. One hell of a fight.

When his sister and her husband are killed in an accident, Aussie cattle station owner Lachlan McCoughney rushes to Texas to rescue their infant daughter, Chloe. He expects to find his niece living in squalor with the Sheffields, a rodeo family.

Instead, Lachlan finds Holden Sheffield, a salt-of-the-earth cowboy running a huge business operation. They want to explore their mutual attraction despite the many problems thrown their way, and together, they must find a way to give Chloe a new family and find a love that spans thousands of acres and two continents.

www.dreamspinnerpress.com

Available Now

ⓓREAMSPUN DESIRES

#1

The Millionaire Upstairs by M.J. O'Shea

He might be hard to work for, but he's impossible to resist.

Sasha Sobieski has the perfect job working at legendary American fashion house Harrison Kingsley—or at least he used to. He just never thought he'd have to work for Harrison Kingsley himself. Harrison is exacting, difficult, cold, and hands-down the sexiest man Sasha has ever seen.

After years at the top, Harrison Kingsley knows what he wants, when he wants it, and exactly how he'd like it to be delivered to him. What he wants most right now? His new assistant. Sasha is mouthy, opinionated, and he drives Harrison mad. Problem is, Harrison can never tell if it's with anger… or desire.

#2

First Comes Marriage by Shira Anthony

Their marriage was supposed to be all business....

When struggling novelist Chris Valentine meets Jesse Donovan, he's interested in a book contract, or possibly a date. The last thing Chris expects is a marriage proposal from New York City's most eligible bachelor!

Jesse's in a pinch. To keep control of his company, he has to marry. So he has valid reasons for offering Chris this business deal: in exchange for living in a gorgeous mansion for a year, playing the doting husband, Chris gets all the writing time he wants and walks away with a million-dollar payoff. Surely Chris can handle that. He can handle living with the most handsome and endearing man he's ever met, a man he immediately knows he wants in the worst way and can't have. Or can he?

Love Always Finds a Way

ⓓREAMSPUN DESIRES
Subscription Service

Love eBooks?

Our monthly subscription service
gives you two eBooks per month for
one low price. Each month's titles
will be automatically delivered
to your Dreamspinner Bookshelf
on their release dates.

Prefer print?

Receive two paperbacks per month!
Both books ship on the 1st of the
month, giving you *exclusive* early
access! As a bonus, you'll receive
both eBooks on their release dates!

Visit
www.dreamspinnerpress.com
for more info or to sign up now!

FOR **MORE** OF THE **BEST GAY ROMANCE**

Made in the USA
Columbia, SC
07 July 2024